MANDALAY

THE UNITED STATES

HAWK'S

OF ANTHROPOCENE

DILEMMA

A middle-grade novel, set in 2030, about global warming
and a young teen's effort to stop it

Peter Aronson

Library of Congress Cataloging-in-Publication Data

ISBN 978-1-7320775-2-2 (ebook)
ISBN 978-1-7320775-3-9 (paper)

Front and back cover designs by Ashley Byland of Redbird Designs
Layout and formatting by Streetlight Graphics

www.peteraronsonbooks.com
Double M Books Inc.: peteraronsonbooks@gmail.com

Dear Sophia, Faith + Doyle:

I hope you enjoy the book +
may it inspire you to
big things.

All the best

Peter Aronson
NYC, 1/24/22

Dedicated to my parents, Herb and Connie Aronson, who encouraged and inspired me to pursue my passion.

And dedicated to my loving and supportive wife, Emily, and to my daughters, Mabel and Maisy, and their generation. They will need a monumental worldwide effort to tackle global warming and all its consequences.

PART 1: GETTING TO KNOW MANDALAY HAWK

The story begins on April 2, 2030, in a small town in Maine.

Chapter 1: The storm that lit the fire

M ANDALAY COULD HEAR AND FEEL the panic in her dad's crackly voice. His last-ditch effort to get emergency supplies before they evacuated had become a nightmare. Through the phone static, she heard him say he wouldn't be able to get home, because police had closed the roads.

There would be no evacuation. Mandalay was stranded alone.

She stood in her living room, staring out the window, seeing what Mother Nature had unleashed on the coast of Maine: The weather experts called it a MaineCane - the biggest hurricane ever to hit Maine - a category 4 storm expected to pack 150 mile per hour winds and dump more than three feet of rain. Trees in Mandalay's yard were already snapping like small twigs. Water from the Back River was rising towards the house. And this was just the start.

Mandalay was 13 and lived alone with her dad, two miles from the closest neighbor.

Mandalay tried calling her father back. All she got was: "I'm sorry, the number you are trying to reach ..."

She clicked off her ring phone as her house shuttered and shook from the wind. She knew she had little time and only one option, because they didn't have a basement or a secure room. She needed to build a fort in the back of the living room, away from the window, a fort that would give her a fighting chance of surviving this storm. She was a strong girl from helping her dad chop wood in the backyard. She went to work.

She pushed and pulled the couch to the back of the room,

then dragged the big chair next to it and tipped it over. Then she dragged her desk, her mattress and the coffee and kitchen tables and tipped them over, creating a sturdy perimeter. She pushed and pulled the dining room table and turned it upside down so it formed a roof. She tied a thick rope around the table and shoved the end of it into the fort. She then put on her dad's rain pants, her heavy boots, gloves and two raincoats and climbed inside and yanked and yanked the table over her head. She didn't recall ever praying in her life before, but she was now.

Within a few minutes, she heard the sharp crack of the living room window, then a howling wind so ear-splittingly loud she could barely hear the glass shattering, the tree limbs smashing through the house and the debris whipping around her.

She had draped a thick blanket over her head and held onto the rope for dear life - the rope that was holding the table in place despite the ferocious winds, holding onto that rope so that an avalanche of torn branches, cracked glass and broken roof didn't cascade down on top of her. She held on for hours, focusing on one simple thing, holding that rope so that she could tell her dad how she kicked butt and survived. She then noticed water was creeping up, now covering the lower part of her legs.

As the wind howled, she heard more cracking, as if something was splitting open. Then something fell ...

The next thing Mandalay remembered was hearing these words: "Our dog's got a scent - *over here!*"

Moments later, Mandalay heard sloshing water, frantic scraping and digging and an electric saw cutting and shouting "Lift it!" and "We got to get her out!" Then she recalled being pulled from under a pile of branches, beams and a cracked dining room table, which all partially lay under three feet of water from the Back River, the river that flooded Mandalay's house. But her head miraculously had remained above water, resting on a broken branch. She was soaking wet, chilled to the bone, with a bruised leg and a huge bump on her head, but she was alive. She blinked at the bright light - and realized that she was looking up at the blue sky and bright sun shining through where their roof used to be.

Then she saw her father.

"You'll be ok, darling, I promise, you'll be ok," he said, as he burst into tears and hugged her tight.

**** **** ****

For Mandalay, the next few days were a blur of doctors, nurses and more people telling her how lucky she was than she would have liked.

You're lucky to be alive.

You're lucky you didn't drown.

You're lucky you only got a concussion and a bruised ankle.

Thousands of people died in the storm.

"How does it feel to be the luckiest girl alive?" a TV reporter asked her. "You were lying under a crumpled roof in flood water for more than 12 hours."

Mandalay really wasn't sure what to say to that. But she knew she wanted to go home and get on with her life.

When Mandalay left the hospital a week later, on April 9, spring had returned. In 2030, this meant sunny and high 80s, and the cleanup was underway.

**** **** ****

Mandalay's life returned to something like normal. They had to live with Uncle Jim, her father's best friend - because they didn't have a house anymore. But, soon after, she was able to return to school, in a walking cast and after her concussion protocol was lifted. She was an eighth-grader at Nagatoon Regional Junior-Senior High School.

The first morning her dad drove her to school it took twice as long as normal because one road had been wiped out by flood waters and a second road was blocked by dozens of downed trees.

"You know dad ..." Mandalay said, as she looked out the car

window at all the damaged houses and buildings. She didn't finish the sentence, as she shook her head and grimaced.

"Yeah, what?" he said, as he gave her a quick glance.

"I don't know," she said, as she continued looking at the flattened buildings and cars turned upside down.

But she did know. In 6th grade, her teacher gave the class a special assignment, to write 500 words on what they thought was the biggest problem in the world. Each student could pick the problem, research it and write about the problem and how to fix it.

After talking about it with her dad, Mandalay decided to write about global warming. Mandalay recalled reading an article in *Environment Kids* that was titled EVERYTHING! The article explained how *EVERYTHING!* was getting worse because of global warming - more people were dirt poor, more people were starving, more people were getting sick and dying, and just about everything else bad was happening a lot more: more floods, more droughts, more forest fires, and of course, more deadly, sudden, extreme weather, like MaineCanes, which hit even if it wasn't hurricane season. And, of course, it was hot. They had summer weather, and it was only early spring.

"Gosh, the world's a mess," she wrote. "Something has to be done."

After she handed in her assignment, Mandalay had decided to take a stand. At lunch that day two years ago, she jumped up on the food counter, alongside that day's hot selection of spaghetti and meatballs, and shouted that everyone had to write to the local congresswoman because "Global warming had to be stopped!" She got so carried away that she didn't realize her sneaker dipped into the large, metal dish of spaghetti, with dozens of students on line waiting to be served lunch.

The letter home that day from the principal said:

> *Dear Mr. Hawk: Although we appreciate Mandalay's enthusiasm for a cause - even if it is a lost cause - she actually violated a Maine health code today and forced us to have to*

throw out much of today's lunch. I informed her that she will have detention after school for a week to think about what she did. Please discuss this with her.

Hubert Bushwick, Principal

"Dad, Bushwick's a bum," Mandalay told her dad, after he read the letter.

"I understand you may not like him, sweetheart, but he is your principal and you did step in the spaghetti."

Mandalay did her detention, and used the time to write letters to members of Congress. She convinced a dozen classmates to write also.

The responses they got all seem to say the same thing: That Congress was doing its best.

But what were they really doing? Mandalay was smart enough to wonder at the time. It was 2028, things were getting worse and not nearly enough was being done to stop global warming, even though it was causing more and more problems around the world.

But Mandalay didn't do anything else. She was in sixth grade, she just went along with the flow.

So now it was two years later, and Mandalay was angry with herself - angry because she had waited until a cat 4 MaineCane, the result of global warming, had killed almost 3,000 people in Maine and almost killed her before realizing she'd have to take the next step.

Chapter 2: The bonfire

A T UNCLE JIM'S HOUSE, THE ping pong table was cleared away in the basement and a small bedroom with a bed and a desk was set up for Mandalay.

"Dad, I'll be downstairs doing my homework," Mandalay said after dinner, night after night.

Mandalay was a good student, so she made sure she did her homework first, as quickly as possible. Then she got to work on her plan.

It took her more than a month. By May 28, Mandalay's ankle was healed and her head felt fine. So that night, when she woke up at 2 am to the soft beep of an alarm, Mandalay got dressed, grabbed her backpack and tiptoed out the basement door. Then she biked the four miles to school, dodging downed trees along the way.

A half hour later, Mandalay opened Mr. Krumley's supply cabinet and removed the school's newest electronic devices, 50 shiny, ultra-thin dweebs - the dweebs with the large black letters on the front that said:

Gift to Nagatoon Regional Junior-Senior High School from Star Power Inc.

Star Power Inc. was the area's largest power company, and the dweebs were the companies' most recent gift to Mandalay's school, the same school that Mandalay moments before had broken into, in the middle of the night, by disengaging the school's laser security system, prying open a window and climbing inside.

With gloved hands and a flashlight, Mandalay made a series of trips from the classroom to outside, carrying a half dozen dweebs at a time as she climbed through the open window. Within a few minutes, she had stacked all 50 dweebs on top of each other in the school parking lot, a single, solitary, tall pile in a dark, empty lot. During her last trip inside, she took a few extra minutes to write on the classroom backboard with the bright red lipstick that she had brought along:

NO ONE SHOULD BE DOING BUSINESS
WITH STAR POWER!!!
THEY CAUSE GLOBAL WARMING --
LIKE ALL POWER COMPANIES
USING FOSSIL FUEL!!!
HOW STUPID CAN WE BE?
IF WE DON'T STOP GLOBAL WARMING
NOW, IT WILL BE TOO LATE!
IT WILL MAKE THE PANDEMIC OF 2020
LOOK LIKE A PICNIC IN THE PARK!!!

Mandalay stood in the middle of the classroom, shined her flashlight on the board, and read what she had written. Then she walked back to the blackboard, wiped sweat off her brow, and added:

ENOUGH IS ENOUGH!!!
THIS CRAP HAS TO STOP!!! NOW!!!

Mandalay read what she had written again, then nodded approvingly to herself. She climbed outside through the window one last time. She removed a small bottle of kerosene and a box of matches from her backpack. She poured the kerosene over the tall stack of dweebs, then took a breath because she knew what she was about to do was extreme … But she was fed up and felt she had no choice. She wanted this act to bring fresh attention to climate change, to shake things up, to motivate other kids in town to take serious action.

She lit a match. She tossed it at the dweebs - and watched the fireworks. A dweeb bonfire erupted, flames and smoke shooting to the sky. Then she hopped on her bike and took off.

Chapter 3: The Big Shaboozle

FIVE HOURS LATER ... MANDALAY walked into her 8th grade class a few minutes before eight.

Right away, she noticed a terrible smell, but didn't want to bring any attention to herself, so she just laid low.

"God, something stinks," one kid said, then another, and another.

For some reason, the window shades in Mr. Krumley's class were down.

A moment later, Mr. Krumley announced, "Apparently, we had an incident last night. As a result, today's math test is postponed." Then Mr. Krumley scratched his head, glanced towards the shaded window, and added: "I'll be back in a few minutes. Please do the assignment on the board."

The class looked at the blackboard.

"What the heck is that?" one kid shouted out.

"Yeah - what the ...?"

Kids cracked up. A dozen sheets of white paper were taped to the blackboard, a pathetic attempt to cover the now-smudged red lipstick message written by Mandalay the night before. On one piece of paper was written the math assignment.

As soon as Mr. Krumley was out the door, kids in the class couldn't rip off the paper on the blackboard fast enough.

The kids were able to read the lipstick message. They shook their heads and laughed.

"Yeah, that company does suck," one boy said.

"Yeah, they totally suck," a girl added, with many others agreeing.

Then one kid ripped open the shades. The entire class looked out the window and saw Principal Bushwick, Mr. Krumley, the

Nagatoon fire chief, the Nagatoon police chief and about half a dozen police officers standing in the hot morning sun, looking at a partially blackened parking lot and the charred remains of 50 dweebs burnt to a crisp. Mandalay knew all too well what had happened, but she kept her mouth shut. She and her classmates saw Principal Bushwick getting angrier and angrier as he surveyed the scene and examined the melted remains.

The class was too stunned to say much. Mandalay just went along with it, staying calm, letting her anonymous deed just speak for itself.

"Someone is messing with my school!" Principal Bushwick shouted angrily to the police and fire chiefs, as he held up a blackened piece of fried dweeb. He then marched into school.

He called the Maine commissioner of education and gave her the bad news. She gave Bushwick an order that made him so mad his face turned the color of a ripe red apple.

Moments later, Principal Bushwick's sweaty, angry face suddenly appeared on the flashblast at the front of all classrooms in the school, followed by his dreaded voice: "As some of you may know, there has been a breach in security - and we now have a toxic smell in our school."

Half the students in Mandalay's class rolled their eyes amidst a chorus of loud *"Duhhhhs!!!"*

"Because of this - this inexcusable act," Principal Bushwick said, pausing, barely able to say the words he was ordered to say, "School is dismissed for the day."

There was a momentary pause between announcement and reaction. Did he just say school was done for the day? Mandalay had pulled off *The Big Shaboozle*, her code name for this caper, a caper she hoped would send shock waves through her town. Mandalay may have been only 13, but she thought big. Kids went crazy with the news of cancelled school and zapped on their ring phones about it all over town.

Mandalay felt fantastic, like she had conquered the world. But not for long.

Chapter 4: The Discovery

MANDALAY WALKED ALL THE WAY home from school, one sweaty mile after another. It was 92 degrees in May. She knew she had done the right thing.

Until she told her dad. Tom Hawk was a liberal-minded social worker. Mandalay didn't have a mom, so she told her dad everything.

"You did what?" her dad said, his eyes becoming much bigger than usual.

And then it was as if another MaineCane slammed into Mandalay. Principal Bushwick swore he'd catch the "criminal" who did this. He interviewed teachers and students. And then he got hold of the footage from the one police camera in town, a camera Mandalay knew nothing about, a camera that clearly showed one very eager 13-year-old girl pedaling her bike awfully fast through downtown Nagatoon - at about 2:15 am one recent night.

"Ok, you caught me," Mandalay blurted out, when Bushwick and the police chief stopped her as she entered school two days later.

Bushwick stared at her, his face muscles tightening as he got angier. Then he raised his hand and pointed his finger.

"You!" he said, his angry voice rising. "You're the one who stepped in the spaghetti. You little *troublemaker!* I can't believe it - *an eighth grader!*" He was turning reddish-purple.

"I'm not going to ask you to explain how or why - or anything, because I don't care! Just gather your things and leave the building at once and ... and ... never, *ever*, return to this school!" He stared at her, nostrils flaring, face getting even more red, if that was possible.

Mandalay stood there for a second, shocked, sweat dripping

down her back. She never realized in a million years that it would be this bad. She hadn't thought it through. She wanted to talk with her dad at that very moment, but she was alone.

Then a crowd began gathering around her and Bushwick in the hallway. She heard a student in the crowd shout: "We love you Mandalay!"

Principal Bushwick heard this, too. Mandalay and Bushwick stared at each other.

Another kid yelled out: "Mandalay, you have guts!"

This gave Mandalay all the nerve she needed. She thought for a second, then said: "That company, Star Power, it's bad for the environment, it's bad for the world. They really suck!"

She couldn't believe she had said that, but she kept going. "Yeah, they really, really suck. And this school should not be supporting that company. Any school that supports a company like that also sucks." She clenched her jaw. "So Nagatoon Junior-Senior High now officially sucks." She was sweating and shaking, but still managed to stare down the principal. "I'll see you later Principal Bushwick." She turned and walked out.

But that night at home it began to sink in. Mandalay had been expelled from school. *As an eighth grader. Didn't even make it to high school. Not too cool.* Her dad shook his head a lot, took a lot of deep breaths and had the most serious look on his face Mandalay had ever seen. He really loved his daughter, *really* loved her a lot. But he didn't have a plan for this. "Well, I'm not sure what we're going to do now, because you can't become a 13-year-old dropout."

It then got worse. A day later, the county prosecutor announced he was going to go after Mandalay Hawk. The angry police chief called Mandalay a "punk hooligan."

Mandalay didn't even know what the word hooligan meant.

Chapter 5: Will Mandalay go to jail, or won't she, that is the question?

A MONTH LATER, MANDALAY HAWK HAD a date at the county courthouse. Mandalay had admitted everything. It was now her day of reckoning.

"All rise," the court clerk shouted, as County Judge Mary Baxter strode into the courtroom, wearing a flowing black robe and quickly stood behind the bench.

"Please be seated," she said, as she looked out at the large crowd: Mandalay and her dad, Prosecutor Wyatt D'Antoni, Principal Bushwick, and dozens of eighth graders there to support Mandalay. Large ceiling fans whirled overhead on another hot day. "Both sides will speak and then I'll announce my decision. Mr. Prosecutor, you may proceed."

Prosecutor D'Antoni rose. "As everyone in the courtroom and the state knows, this girl, this 13-year-old troublemaker, Mandalay Hawk" - pointing an accusing finger at her - "committed a serious crime that caused thousands of dollars in damage and caused the school to close its doors for three days because of a toxic odor. She acted on her own and she's shown no remorse. She hasn't apologized and she hasn't uttered those magic words, *'I made a mistake, I shouldn't have done it, I was wrong and I'm sorry.'* "

"Hey, why should I apologize for doing something I think was right?" Mandalay shouted, as she jumped to her feet. "And look at the positive ..."

"You see, Your Honor, she's shown no remorse, none whatsoever," the prosecutor said angrily, cutting her off. "She'd just do it again and again. We request that she be punished for the serious crime she committed, that she be taught a lesson. She should spend a year in junior juvie jail, at Beaver Creek Detention Facility, near the Canadian border. That will teach her a lesson."

"*What?!*" Mandalay shouted. "*A year where?!*"

Mandalay's father stood up and placed a comforting hand on Mandalay's shoulder. "Darling, please," he urged in a whisper.

"Your honor, I'm Mandalay's father, Tom Hawk. She doesn't understand that what she did was very wrong. She's only 13 and ..."

"Baloney dad!" Mandalay interrupted. "I knew exactly what I was doing and you know it."

"Mandalay, please," he said quietly to her, taking a deep breath.

"Ms. Hawk," Judge Baxter said sternly, "didn't you realize that doing all that damage was terribly wrong?"

Mandalay shook her head. "No! What's wrong is global warming and Star Power is making it worse. What are we supposed to do - use their dumb dweebs like nothing is going on?"

The judge took a deep breath, seeing a smart – *very smart* – and determined handful right in front of her. She knew darn well that this kid was right, that global warming had to be stopped, but bonfires in the parking lot was not the way to do it.

"But Ms. Hawk, the question is: Did you ever consider that what you did was wrong – as in - *illegal?*" the judge asked. "There are other ways ..."

"No, your honor," Mandalay interrupted. "I consider what I did an act of civil disobedience."

"Go Mandalay!" a classmate shouted.

The judge banged her gavel so hard and loud it seemed to shake the room.

"Quiet in the courtroom – and I mean that!" an angry Judge Baxter shouted, as she looked out at all the kids packed into her courtroom. Then she looked at Mandalay.

"Ms. Hawk, civil disobedience doesn't involve breaking and entering and destroying school property," the judge explained.

"So, you need to be taught a lesson. A lesson so that you never do anything like this again. First off, Mr. Hawk, I am ordering you to pay the Nagatoon school district $50,000 for the damage your daughter did. She's your daughter - you lost control of her, you pay the price."

"Dad!" an angry and worried Mandalay gasped.

Tom Hawk shook his head and took a deep breath. He didn't expect that.

"It's ok dear," Tom Hawk whispered, distressed, but trying to remain calm, so he could focus on keeping his daughter out of juvie.

"As for you, Ms. Hawk," Judge Baxter proclaimed. "We need to address ..."

"Your honor, may I speak?" Tom Hawk interrupted, realizing he needed to speak now, before it was too late.

"Of course, that's your right before I sentence your daughter. Go ahead."

Mandalay's father nervously removed a piece of paper from his pants pocket.

"Judge Baxter," Tom Hawk began, his voice quivering with emotion, "it ... it's important that you know a little about Mandalay before you make your decision. I know sometimes my daughter does things she shouldn't do ... and ... and yes, she really messed up here. But your honor, you need to understand what she's been through." His lips quivered as he tried to control his emotions. He paused to gather himself and wiped sweat from his brow.

"She ... she comes from somewhere in Idaho – *somewhere*. I don't even know where exactly, because the adoption agency refused to tell me. But they did tell me this: In the year before I became Mandalay's father, she was shuttled from one foster home to another. Her mother couldn't take care of her. She ran away from three foster homes. She was caught stealing food several times. No other foster home would take her. So her mother took her back – and then put her up for adoption through a special agency that dealt with troubled kids. Mandalay was seven at the time - *seven*," Tom Hawk said, his voice cracking with emotion.

"The agency called me the day I posted on the net that I was looking to adopt. I'm a social worker and I had run a homeless shelter in the past. They figured we'll let this guy handle this problem kid, because we don't know what else to do with her.

"A few weeks later, I picked up Mandalay. We drove for a long time in silence. This beautiful, wonderful, angry young girl, she just sat there. Wouldn't say a word. So I asked her why she stole food. And do you know what she said?"

The judge, emotion welling up, shook her head.

"She said her foster families didn't feed her enough - so she was always hungry. *She was just a hungry girl.* So at the next exit, I pulled off and found the nearest diner and we had our first meal together. She ate fried chicken. Then she ate French toast. And then she ate chocolate cream pie. And then a pickle and ice cream. I'll never forget that meal. She actually scooped up ice cream on the pickle and ate it. She said she had always wanted to eat ice cream that way, with a pickle as a spoon – *a pickle spoon*, she called it - but she had never been given the chance. Between bites, she told me she liked to read. And she told me that she just wanted to sleep in the same bed until her next birthday. That was her goal. When I told her that I wasn't a foster parent and that I wasn't a temporary parent, she said: 'You're a liar, mister.' And then she didn't speak to me for the next four days – the rest of the ride to Maine and the first two days in our home. She ate everything I put on the table, but she wouldn't say a word. Until I gave her a present. I bought her a book, Shel Silverstein's *The Giving Tree*. I wrote on the inside cover:

> *Dear Mandalay: I'm not a pretend father. I'm the real deal. I promise to take care of you forever. Forever and Ever. I Love You, dad*

"She must have stared at those words for 10 minutes. I remember every second of those 10 minutes. *Every second.* It was almost as if she was staring at those words to see if they would disappear. As she stared, she continued to stuff macaroni and cheese into her mouth.

"Then she stopped eating and said simply, 'Ok, dad, want to read with me?' Then we sat on the couch and read Shel Silverstein's poems. And that's how this family began."

The judge had tears in her eyes, and Tom Hawk had a small flood on his face.

Principal Bushwick was shaking his head.

Tom Hawk wiped his face with a tissue.

"Your honor," he continued, sniffling, "Mandalay Hawk has already done her time in juvie jail - by being shipped from one foster home to another. In fact, foster homes, with not enough food and no love, are much worse than jail. Locking her up somewhere won't do any good. Give her a chance to channel her energy in a positive way – and well, she could change the course of something. I don't know what. But something."

The judge looked at Tom Hawk, then at Mandalay ... thinking ...

"Thank you, Mr. Hawk," Judge Baxter finally said. "Ms. Hawk ... my ... my ..."

The judge paused. She was wondering - *what to do with this kid?* She looked down, then around, then out into the courtroom. She was trying to figure out her next move. She took a deep breath, then sat up straight in her chair and looked directly at Mandalay.

"Ok," Judge Baxter finally said. "Ms. Hawk, making a decision can be difficult when your heart and mind tell you two different things. My mind says, very strongly, that you must be taught a lesson. Otherwise, you'll probably break the law again. But my heart says, give this kid a second chance - because her intentions are good."

Mandalay didn't know judges could be so honest in court.

"Ms. Hawk, I'm putting you on probation. I'll wipe your record clean if you don't get kicked out of school and you don't break the law in the next year. You must accomplish both things. If you don't comply - I'll send you to junior juvie jail in the deep, dark woods of Maine for much longer than you could ever imagine. And I don't give a hoot that because of your illegal act, there's been some new publicity about fighting global warming. There's a right way to protest and a wrong way - and you chose the wrong, very destructive, way. Got that?"

The judge stared at Mandalay.

'Yes … yes, your honor," said a shaky, but relieved Mandalay.

"Don't break into any more buildings," Judge Baxter warned. "Don't light any more bonfires. But break some boundaries. Shatter some. I hope I never see you again in my courtroom. The $50,000 is due in 60 days." The judge shot a serious look at Mr. Hawk, then smashed her gavel down on the bench.

"Court adjourned," she commanded, then rose and exited the courtroom.

Mandalay took a deep breath. "Jeez dad, that was awfully close," she sighed quietly.

"Yeah, too close," he sighed back, "way too close."

PART 2: THE EPIC STORY BEGINS

Chapter 1: A New World

As they sped down the highway, Mandalay opened her car window wide so the wind hit her smack in the face. It was either that, or practically suffocate. The AC in their car had conked out a few years back, after it began getting a lot warmer. That was in 2025. Now, it was fall 2030, and it was even hotter.

Mandalay and her father were heading south, south to a new life in New York City.

"You need a fresh start, where you're no longer The BTOC - The Big Troublemaker On Campus," Mandalay's dad had told her, only half smiling. "If you can't blend in in New York City, where can you?"

Mandalay finished her eighth-grade school work at Uncle Jim's in Maine over the summer. It took her dad until October to sell the house, but once he did, he paid the court fine of $50,000 and they took off.

They followed their car's GPS to New York, but it failed to tell them that some roads to the city had been wiped out by floods and forest fires. They followed detours and saw the damage that was done.

Both sides of the Saw Mill River Parkway had been burnt to a crisp. The road was lined with charred trees and blackened homes and buildings that had burned to the ground. A devastated gas station looked like a bomb had hit it. A motel had a long line of charred rooms that were about three feet tall, with no walls or ceilings.

"Jeez, this is scary," Mandalay said, shaking her head, trying not to think too much about the global warming that had led to all this destruction.

Her mood suddenly brightened when she saw a long row of palm trees as they neared New York City. "Wow, I love them," she said, as they cruised down the highway. "I didn't expect that, but aren't they supposed to be in the tropics?"

"Yeah, I think so," her dad said. "They grow in really warm weather."

"Hmm," Mandalay said, her smile fading, realizing what she was seeing.

The closer they got to New York, the hotter and stickier it got.

That night, they moved into their tiny two-bedroom apartment in the Morningside Heights section of Manhattan, in New York City.

At dinner, Mandalay's dad reminded her why they had left Maine and that she would be starting at a new school - *high school* - where no one knew her. "Remember sweetheart, play it cool, ok? Lay low and please follow the rules - because Judge Baxter is hanging over your head. I don't want you getting in any trouble, understand?"

"Sure dad," Mandalay said, as she tried real hard not to roll her eyes at her father.

After dinner, she locked herself in the bathroom and took a cool bath, because it was steamy hot in the apartment. She also did something else.

The next morning, when her dad saw her, he sighed loudly, shook his head and said only one word: "*Why?*"

Mandalay tried to contain her smile.

"Why not dad, come on."

Her dad was staring at her, as she got ready to leave for her first day of high school in what they both jokingly called the *Big Bad City*.

Mandalay had dyed her long brown hair bright orange.

"Just having fun dad, jeez." She kissed her dad on the cheek.

"Will you please watch yourself on the streets. This isn't Maine, you know."

"Yeah, I heard New York is a little different." She rolled her eyes playfully.

"You know where you're going?"

"Yup, GPSed it. Ten blocks south."

She snapped up her backpack. "Love ya, dad - see ya." She was out the door before he could say another word.

**** **** ****

On her first day at Ernest Hemingway High School, Mandalay met her two new friends.

Before math class, she met Jazmin.

"I love your shirt," a smiling Mandalay said, pointing to Jazmin's **Girls Rule the World - REALLY!!!** t-shirt, as she approached her.

"My mom says it's true," Jazmin said, returning the smile.

"Oh, yeah, I know it's true," Mandalay said, smiling back, playfully holding up a clenched fist.

"I love your hair," Jazmin said, pointing at the flowing orange do. "Are you new?"

"Oh yeah, brand new," Mandalay said, smiling, nodding.

They sat next to each other in class. About five minutes in, Jazmin mouthed the words, "*I'm bored already.*" Mandalay cracked up and gave Jazmin a thumbs up.

Three hours later, Mandalay met her second friend.

Jazmin took Mandalay out for lunch to a place that Mandalay didn't know existed.

"Wow, this is amazing," Mandalay said, shaking her head in wonder. She was staring at a gleaming white, double-decker boat bobbing in the water - actually bobbing in a canal that had been carved right through the middle of New York City.

"The canals are new," Jazmin explained. "They had to build them because of all that global warming flooding - you know, the rising seas, the hurricanes, the rainblasts. The water kept on coming."

"Oh yeah, heard about that flooding," Mandalay said, nodding casually, not wanting to let on what she really knew about the environmental emergency the earth now faced.

They ate rice-seaweed wraps as they sailed through Central Park, past palm trees and houseboats lining the canal.

"This is fun," Mandalay said, as the boat wound its way through the heart of New York.

Then Mandalay noticed some guy sitting on the edge of the boat, his feet propped up on deck, reading a book.

"That guy's gonna fall in if he's not careful," Mandalay said.

Jazmin looked over, then did a double take.

"Oh God," she moaned.

"You know him?" Mandalay asked.

"Unfortunately, yeah. He's in our grade." Jazmin rolled her eyes.

"He looks kind of cool," Mandalay said, eyeing his extra-puffy fro and bright green sneakers. "Let's go talk to him."

"Oh, no, you don't want to do that," Jazmin insisted. "He's one weird dude."

"How weird can he be?" Mandalay asked.

"Well, darn weird. I've known him for a month, since ninth grade started. He doesn't talk. He doesn't socialize. All he does is read. His real name is McKenzie Patooma, but he wants everyone to call him some other weirdo name."

Mandalay was off before Jazmin knew what had happened.

"Hi, I'm Mandalay and I'm new at Hemingway High," Mandalay blurted out, leaning forward. "You don't want to fall in, do you?" She eyed the water under his dangling feet.

The guy ignored Mandalay, didn't look up from his book, didn't stop reading, didn't acknowledge her in any way.

Mandalay shrugged at Jazmin.

"I told you," Jazmin whispered to Mandalay. "Weeir-do," she mouthed.

"So McKenzie, what do you like to be called?" Mandalay pushed, trying another angle, as the boat continued sailing through Central Park, passing a police boat and kayakers.

This question caught his attention. He shook his head, slowly put down his book (*Zeitoun,* by Dave Eggers), turned his head and looked Mandalay square in the face. He noticed the orange hair, paused and squinted a little, then said, "Gute's my name, because that's what my dad likes to call me. Now, do you mind?" He shook his head again and resumed reading.

"So, why does your dad like to call you Gute?" Mandalay persisted, with now even Jazmin shaking her head at Mandalay's insistence.

He put his book down again. He sighed and shook his head. "Jeez, you are a nosy one, aren't you? I don't even know you."

"Just trying to make friends," Mandalay said, shrugging.

"Yeah, well, if you must know - I used to be a tech guy ... uhm, well, really a tech *idiot* - ok?" he said. "I was addicted to everything - my ring, my dweeb, blah, blah. Like you two, *right?* Then my dad got angry and said I had to start reading books, or he would throw all my devices in the dumpster. He forced me to read a book about Johannes Gutenberg. You know, the guy who invented the printing press. Totally changed my life. Then I began reading - *a lot.* I ditched all my devices. Sounds crazy, but it's true."

Gute shrugged self-consciously. "Then my dad started calling me Gute, short for Gutenberg. So that's the story. Ok? Have you heard enough?" He raised his eyebrows, cocked his head.

Mandalay shook her head. "Yeah, wow, that's insane. Jeez, you're different, that's for sure."

Even Jazmin was impressed. "If I only knew all this before," Jazmin said, sounding apologetic. "I wouldn't have thought you were so weird. I mean, you're still kind of weird, but ..." She smiled at him. "But cool-weird, which is ok."

Gute shrugged. "Yeah, well ... No one's ever asked before. Certainly no one with orange hair." He rolled his eyes, picked up his book, flicked to the page he was on ... but then put it down again. He did not resume reading.

There was silence for a minute. They all looked out on the canal, water rippling against the stone wall, sea gulls lazily flying by. Mandalay was loving this ride on her first day of school.

"This sure beats driving everywhere and it sure beats being in class," she said.

"Class?" Jazmin blurted out, as the boat pulled into a dock. Jazmin glanced at her watch.

"Oh jeez!" she shouted, alarmed. She flashed them her watch.

School resumed at 1. It was 1:15. They had sailed all the way across town to the East River, a mile from school.

Chapter 2: Are you kidding me?

MANDALAY WAS TOO FLUSTERED TO think about what was happening: It was her first day of school and already she had to go to the principal's office.

When they entered, Mandalay first stared, then blinked, then squinted to focus her eyes. Then she shook her head, blinked again and tried to refocus. She wondered if what she saw was a mirage, a delusion or a nightmare - about a school on the dark side of hell.

Because standing in front of her was Principal Bushwick.

Not possible, Mandalay thought.

"Good afternoon. Please sit down," Principal Bushwick said.

Did the word please just come out of Principal Bushwick's mouth? Mandalay wondered.

"I know starting at a new school can be jarring. Mandalay, are Jazmin and uhm, you know, uhm, what's-his-name - are they helping you get adjusted?"

Mandalay looked at this man – the man who just a few months earlier had expelled her from her Maine school for life. *How could this be?* He appeared different, nicer – with no apparent memory of their past.

"Principal Bushwick ... " Mandalay blurted out, then paused. "Uhm ... what's going on here?"

Jazmin and Gute looked at Mandalay. They both had just met Mandalay, didn't know her at all. But they still wondered what she was talking about.

Principal Bushwick was puzzled as well. "Well, Mandalay, I'm not sure what you mean. In any event, Mandalay, Jazmin and yes, uhm, McKenzie - is that your name? Please try to get to class on time. You'll see less of me, more of your teachers, and we'll all be better for it, right?"

Principal Bushwick scribbled on the late pad, and then tore off three slips, one for each of them.

"Here, give these to Mr. Ledbetter. I'm sure he'll be happy to see you. And remember, an on-time student is a happy student."

Oh jeez, Mandalay thought, *did he really just say that?* Bushwick used to say those exact same words in Maine, too.

Mandalay was in shock.

Did Principal Bushwick have amnesia? He was not the type of principal, not the kind of person, to let bygones be bygones. No way. *He would sooner rip Mandalay's guts out.*

Mandalay was so shocked she felt dizzy as she rose to her feet. As she reached for the principal's outstretched hand and took the slip, she noticed something: A scar on the principal's forehead. A long, thin scar running across, above his eyebrows. She never noticed the scar before. She wondered if Bushwick had a frontal lobotomy over the summer, just to erase Mandalay from his memory, and now, as principal of this new school, had no recall of her? There was no other explanation.

Then she noticed something else. A photo on the wall. She walked over so she could take a closer look, a photo of Principal Bushwick with another man, with someone else who looked very familiar. And looked just like Principal Bushwick.

"Who's that?" Mandalay asked, pointing at the photo. "That person standing next to you – who's *that*?"

"Oh, that's my dear, twin brother, Hubert. Just so happens, he's a school principal, too - in Maine," Principal Bushwick said, as Mandalay stared in disbelief.

Mandalay took a deep breath, still staring at the photo. "So there are two of you?"

"My mother always said we were two peas in a pod, Hubert and Homer, and she wasn't kidding," Principal Bushwick said, proudly. "My brother loves kids even more than I do. What a great guy he is. I love him dearly."

Mandalay was breathing evenly, focusing, trying not to hyper-ventilate. She felt sweat trickling down her back. *Oh brother*, she could not believe her luck. She had to remain calm.

Mandalay didn't say anything about this to Jazmin or Gute. Her past was the past. And she planned, hoped, prayed ... on keeping it that way.

Chapter 3: Getting to know each other

OVER THE NEXT WEEK OR SO, Mandalay, Gute and Jazmin became fast friends. They matched New York's rainbow diversity. Mandalay was about five-two with orange hair and light brown skin. Jazmin, five-nine, had super-long, jet-black hair and bronze skin. And Gute was over six foot and had dark brown skin and that big afro that made him look like a giant. They quickly found common ground, first through a deal: Gute agreed to socialize so they could all hang together, as long as Mandalay and Jazmin agreed to go no tech. This meant they couldn't use their rings - those devices that had replaced cell phones about five years ago. They put their rings in their pockets and started doing something most kids their age didn't do: They started talking to each other - face to face.

For lunch one day, they ate kale wraps and walked in Central Park.

"So what's your backstory?" Mandalay asked Gute, between bites, curious about this kid.

"My story's my story, you know," he shrugged. "I live with my dad. I don't have a mom. My dad's from Kenya - he's the best. My mom, I don't know - I think she was from Asia or somewhere." He half smiled and shrugged again. "Not sure and don't care. My parents got divorced when I was like five. My mom ... *puuhh*." He just waved his hand and shook his head.

Mandalay and Jazmin nodded sympathetically.

They strolled past one sandy field after another filled with large cactus trees. They drank lots of water and mopped sweat off their faces with their stink towels, the latest new craze, used dish towels people carried around to wipe sweat off their face.

"I guess we all have some mystery in us," Mandalay said. "My adopted dad is the best, too. I only knew my bio mom, but not for too long. I hardly remember her. She dumped me on the side of the road in Idaho like a rotten banana. She just put me up for adoption. She said: 'I don't want you anymore. See ya.' " Mandalay laughed out loud, but kind of felt sad.

"And my bio dad" - she laughed again - "all I know is, he probably wasn't as lily white as my mom." She was pointing at her arm, showing off her light brown skin. "I don't know. Maybe someday I'll find out."

"Gosh, we do have a lot in common," Jazmin said. "I was born in Morocco, but my dad dropped dead when I was like two, so my mom brought me to America. I don't remember him at all." Jazmin shrugged, shaking her head.

The three of them looked at each other. Mandalay patted Jazmin on the back, Gute nodded sympathetically.

"That must be kind of hard, knowing for sure your dad's not here anymore," Mandalay said.

Jazmin shrugged. "Kind of. But I never really knew him."

They walked quietly through Central Park, thinking about what they had just said to each other. Three peas in one-parent pods, with absent or dead parents.

It was a hot October day. They guzzled from their water bottles.

They came upon a small field with freshly cut grass. The sign at the entrance said:

We water this field twice a day to keep it green, like it was 2025. Enjoy the grass.

They lay down and breathed in the wonderful, grassy, earthy smell.

"This reminds me of Maine when I first got there - before it got so hot," Mandalay said. "We had a green lawn and my dad used to mow it and I would just lie down in the grass, close my eyes and inhale. Then it got brown and disgusting."

"I almost forgot. We're becoming fast friends with a country girl," Gute said, smiling.

They looked up at the lazy white clouds drifting by. Gute threw a few blades of grass in the air and watched them flitter in the breeze. Then Gute picked up a handful of fresh cut grass, sat up and threw it at Mandalay. Then he picked up a second handful and threw it at Jazmin.

"Grass fight!" he shouted, as he stood up and grabbed more and more grass and heaved it at both of them.

"Hey, I thought you were this shy, quiet bookface," Jazmin teased, as she dodged the grass.

"Well, I used to be," Gute said, as he grabbed and threw more grass.

They tossed grass all over each other. By the time they were done, exhausted and sweaty, they were all covered in wet, sticky grass. They brushed themselves off.

Then they bought ice cream cones and resumed walking, past palm trees and cactus fields. Then Gute asked Mandalay, "So why did you move here from Maine?"

This question caught Mandalay off guard. She was momentarily flustered. "Well, uhm, you see, my dad - well, he, uhm, he got a new job. So he said, 'We're moving.' It was, uhm, really that simple. He runs a senior center across town." Mandalay nodded. She hated lying, not telling the whole truth. But she and her dad had agreed that her past was the past, that she was moving on, not telling anyone what had happened.

But she really, really liked her new friends, and she hated not telling them why she really moved to New York. *Hated it.*

They walked for a minute or two. Gute looked at his watch.

"Shhhhhooot!" he shouted. "It's 1:20!"

They had lost track of time - *again*.

**** **** ****

"Congratulations on abusing and losing your lunch-out privilege so early in the year," were the first words Principal Bushwick said to them, stern-faced, with hands on hips. Gone was Principal Mr. Nice Guy. "I've seen the three of you now twice within two weeks. That's one too many times." He was shaking his head. "When lunch ends at one, that means one."

They were standing in a row, in front of their angry principal.

"Remember, this is high school. Rules are rules. For the next month, you're not allowed out for lunch."

Jazmin glanced at her friends, wondering why Bushwick was being so nasty all of sudden.

"You're dismissed - except for you," he said, staring and pointing at Mandalay. "I want to talk to you."

Gute and Jazmin looked at their new friend, wondering what was going on, as a shiver shot up and down Mandalay's spine - a shiver all the way from Maine.

"Shut the door behind you," Bushwick ordered Jazmin and Gute, as they walked out.

Mandalay was sweating bullets, wondering what was going on.

Once the door was closed: "I know who you are!" Bushwick blurted out angrily, which explained why he had gone from nice to nasty in a snap. "And I know that you know who I am. So I'll be very, very, *very* clear. I'm not going to tolerate any of your nonsense."

Mandalay could hardly talk. "How … how do you …"

"How do I know?" he interrupted angrily. "My brother called me yesterday. Your father had to tell the court which school you would attend. The prosecutor shared the news with my brother."

Bushwick stared daggers at Mandalay. "When my brother found out you landed here, he almost fell through the floor. You messed with him big time. Caused him a lot of stress. You're already starting to mess with me. Bad idea. You better not screw up - or else. Understand?"

Chapter 4: Well, well, well – look who's visiting

MANDALAY COULD NOT BELIEVE THIS. *What were the odds? ... Two Bushwicks ... And now both were out to get her.* There was one - and only one - thought burning through Mandalay's brain: *If I mess up, I'm dead.*

When Gute and Jazmin asked her what was up with Bushwick, Mandalay lied and said, "Oh gosh. Because I'm new here, he gave me an extra warning. What a butthole."

After school, Mandalay speed walked around the neighborhood for a while ... thinking - *really thinking* - about what to do: *Tell her dad, or not?*

"Hi sweetheart, did you run home?" Tom Hawk asked, looking at his sweaty daughter, as she walked through the front door.

"Nope, just walkin' fast and it's hot," she said, managing a fake half smile.

She hated confrontations with her dad. Fortunately, she smelled a delicious home cooked meal waiting for her when she entered the apartment, but then almost fell over when she saw two unexpected guests in their teeny, tiny living room.

She closed her eyes and squeezed them shut. Then opened them, hoping, praying it was a temporary delusion. It wasn't. She looked at her father.

"I thought you would be happy to see some old friends," her dad said, a big, broad smile on his face.

Standing there, sipping glasses of wine, were Principal Bushwick – *the first one!* – and Judge Baxter, the one and only.

"Dad!" was the only word Mandalay could utter. She took a breath to try to calm herself - and stop from fainting.

"So nice to see you," said Principal Bushwick, smiling, not sneering.

"Yes, Mandalay, it was nice of your dad to invite us down from Maine," said Judge Baxter. "You seemed surprised. He didn't tell you we'd be staying a few nights?"

Mandalay couldn't speak any more. She was in shock.

Tom Hawk's grin was even wider now. Then it grew wider ... and wider ... so wide that it swallowed the entire room ... and Mandalay felt dizzy ... dizzier ... and then she woke up, startled upright, swimming in sweat, delirious with fear.

Oh gosh ... she was hyperventilating, having a panic attack.

Mandalay's mind was somersaulting through what had just happened. She shook her head, tried to clear her thoughts, make sense of it all ...

She had just had a really, really, *really* scary dream.

Bushwick #1 and Judge Baxter weren't actually in her apartment.

Mandalay now got it: This is what happens when something bad happens and you don't tell your dad.

Chapter 5: The Big Palm Tree ... and The Big Heat

MANDALAY CALMED DOWN AND TRIED to forget about the Bushwick brothers. She didn't tell her dad there were two of them and that they were out to get her, and she didn't tell Gute and Jazmin about her past.

She just knew she needed to stay calm, keep her mouth shut and stay out of trouble. She became a 9th grade goody, goody two-shoes - she went to school, did her homework, tried to forget all about global warming and didn't raise a ruckus of any kind. She palled around with Gute and Jazmin. Weeks passed. They had fun, like normal 13-year-old kids, enjoying summer in the fall.

One day after school, they rented a triple kayak. Mandalay, Gute and Jazmin doused themselves with Killer Sunspray and put on their floppy sunhats. They paddled east crosstown in the 79th Street canal, passing a floating restaurant and boat bikers. They goofed around, splashing each other. All three got soaked, but they didn't care. Because it was 94 degrees in mid-November and the sun was blazing.

Then they paddled south in the East River, then turned west onto the 59th Street Grand Canal, which cut through the heart of New York City. The Grand Canal was lined with giant palm trees, instead of the Plaza Hotel and all those fancy apartment buildings, which had all been torn down to make room for the canal.

New York City now looked a lot like Venice, Italy, because NYC was now a city carved by zig zagging canals. Water taxis, water buses and houseboats were the norm. Where NYC differed from Venice, however, was with all those cactus gardens and palm trees. New York City, once known as The Big Apple, was now called The Big Palm Tree. New Yorkers had grown to love the palm trees and the canals. And New Yorkers - and most Americans - had grown to enjoy the hotter weather. They certainly were sick of worrying about all the problems it caused. Everyone just went along, like there was nothing wrong with cooking the earth. Mandalay, Gute and Jazmin paddled out of the canal and then went north in the Hudson River. Mandalay then saw something she had not seen before - thousands of New Yorkers swimming and rafting in the Hudson, all the way up to the George Washington Bridge. *In November.*

"This is amazing," Mandalay said to her friends, forgetting, for the moment, *why* it was so hot. "I had no idea. I'm jumping in." She dove into the clear, cool water. Her friends were right behind her.

"Here I come!" Gute yelled, as he stood up and did a belly flop into the Hudson.

"You're not leaving me here!" screamed Jazmin, as she jumped in.

"This is great!" Mandalay shouted, as she treaded water. She and her friends didn't care that they were swimming in their clothes. "How come I didn't know about this?"

Mandalay did a lazy backstroke and saw the George Washington Bridge shimmering in the distance. Sail boats glided by.

Jazmin dove deep under water and surprised Gute with river seaweed smack in the face.

"Got you, got you!" screamed a delirious Jazmin. "This feels sooo good!"

They enjoyed the cool water and the hot sun, with Thanksgiving not too far off.

They finally corralled their kayak and returned to shore. It was late afternoon, the sun was starting to dip. The temperature had dropped to 89. They dripped their way to the subway, so they could head uptown. The subways still ran, under the canals, north and south in the city. But people tried to avoid them. When it was hot outside, the platforms became steamy hot ... and the trains were even hotter, because the AC had stopped working.

The subway car was mostly empty. Mandalay, Gute and Jazmin sat a few feet apart, in this underground sauna. Their soggy clothes got soggier, sweat soaking through. The train sat in the station for a few minutes, then chugged a few stops. Then stopped. Then jerked forward. Then stopped again. They guzzled water and wiped sweat with their smelly stink towels.

The longer they sat on the subway, the hotter Mandalay got. And the hotter she got, the more she began to think and steam and realize what an idiot she had been: *She had allowed herself to enjoy this hot weather. How could she do that?*

Then the lights went out and the emergency lights flicked on, creating even a gloomier, bleaker scene. Mandalay shook her head again - at the situation and at *herself* - as sweat dripped down her face, neck and back.

"Damn subway!" a woman at the far end of the subway car shouted. "What the ..."

Then the large fan overhead that had been blowing hot air around stopped. The stifling, steamy air got hotter.

"I don't like this!" the woman shouted again. "It's a damn sauna!"

Well, yeah, it was a sauna, like trying to breath through a thick, wet sock smothering your face. Mandalay glanced at Gute and Jazmin. They all shook their heads at each other, too miserable to talk, too hot to think, dripping sweat like a warm trickle from a faucet - 110 degrees in a sealed, metal box.

Mandalay felt her breathing becoming labored, a combination of the heat and her rising anxiety. But she was unable to tell her friends what was on her mind - unable to spill the beans because it was a long, long story - a story she promised her dad she would keep to herself.

But then came the cruncher, the words that did break the camel's back, words from an old man who looked and sounded like an old-time preacher, or no, perhaps more like God: "You know, this is *The Big One*," said the man, with a long gray beard and scraggly white hair, sitting directly across from them. "This is *it.*" He spoke with a deep, dark voice, staring ahead with his dark brown eyes.

Mandalay thought he looked awfully creepy.

"You looking at me like I'm crazy," the man said, staring and pointing at Mandalay. "I'm not crazy. Why do you think it's so hot outside in November? Why do you think this subway is a sauna on wheels? This ain't no coincidence. This here's *The Big Heat – The Biiiig Heat!*"

Mandalay had not heard that term before.

"Are you talking about global warming, or something else?" she had to ask.

"Well, *The Biiiig Heat* is the evolution of calamitous environmental and meteorological circumstances, all caused by me, you and eight billion of our best friends," the man said, staring at them. He took a long sip of water from his bottle, then poured the rest over his head.

This made him look even scarier, as water dripped from his matted hair and beard. "It's now about to get much worse than just simple old global warming," he continued with his doomsday talk. "This extreme heat was not predicted, but it came about because our planet just couldn't take it anymore, hit its tipping point. After decades of excessive and increasing carbon emissions, the continuous buildup of greenhouse gases in the atmosphere, coupled with the melting ice shelves, warming seas, etcetera, etcetera, etcetera.

"So now it's late 2030, and we have *The Biiiig Heat*, the *new* global warming: Extensive, extended, extreme heat waves caused by this global turbulence. A jarring upset of earth's environmental balance. It's gonna feel like summer this winter - *all winter*. You'll see. And the problems this heat is causing and will cause - *phew!*" He violently shot his hand through the air.

"I'll be dead, rotting in my grave, before it gets so hot humans can't stand it anymore. I can't say the same for the three of you." He pointed right at Mandalay, Gute and Jazmin.

Mandalay knew this man was a bit crazy. After all, who else would be riding the subway in this weather ranting about *The Big Heat*?

"And I know what I'm talking about. I taught at Harvard for 40 years as a geological climatologist. They gave me a Nobel Prize. I testified before Congress 23 times. They didn't listen. No one listens. They're a bunch of MO-rons."

Mandalay knew this man was right. She wanted to scream. Her brain freeze had thawed, melted in this subway sauna. She drilled into her situation - her dilemma: *Global warming was surrounding her, gearing up to kill everything in its path, and her hands were tied. She was the moron - she had just gone with the flow.*

Mandalay shook her head noticeably as she thought about all this ... and thought about the Bushwick brothers ... and Judge Baxter. She clenched her teeth in anger.

Gute and Jazmin noticed Mandalay had crossed her arms and had this weird, intense scowl on her face. A look they had never seen before.

She appeared to be thinking long and hard about something, but they had no clue.

Chapter 6: Mandalay's Dilemma, #1

A WEEK PASSED. IT SEEMED TO get hotter every day. Sauna in the city, that's what 95 in the shade feels like. When Mandalay walked to school, within one block she was sweating and within two blocks her shirt began sticking to her back. She noticed more and more homeless people with the same sign:

need money for a bottle of water

She hadn't seen that before.

She gave away so much lunch money on the way to school that Mandalay had a running tab at Hemingway High with the lunch lady.

At school, the AC stopped working and the fans were so overworked that they screeched and creaked as they blew hot, stale, smelly air across the classroom.

When Gute and Jazmin asked Mandalay if she wanted to go swimming in the Hudson again a few days later, she said, "Thanks guys, I've got a sore throat. Go without me."

She lied. She didn't have a sore throat. She went to the local library to do some reading. She Shmoogled: *What will it be like to live in New York City in 2050? What is The Big Heat?*

The first article to pop up began like this: "The first question to be answered is: Will New York City still exist in 2050? It may or may not be under water. It depends on several factors."

Mandalay sat in the library and read the article. Then she read some articles about *The Big Heat*, how this new ultra-worldwide heat would speed up global warming even faster than scientists had predicted. She got a gnawing, churning, burning feeling in her stomach, a feeling she had not had in some time. Perhaps not since May, not since that night when she torched those dweebs.

She sat at a table in the library and stared off into space.

The situation, the dilemma, was starting to brew in her mind. Mandalay took a deep, deep breath, then exhaled. *She knew she could not tell anyone what she was thinking. She couldn't tell Gute or Jazmin because #1, they would think she was nuts, and #2, they really didn't know Mandalay Hawk, didn't know her deep down inside. And if she told her dad what she was thinking, he might lock her in her room for the next five years.*

Mandalay knew she couldn't make the same mistake she made in Maine. She decided to read articles about the student protests from 2019 through 2022. She read them … and then she read them again.

Three Million Kids March on Washington, the headline from 2022 blared. *How could they have failed?* Mandalay wondered, shaking her head. *Why didn't the world listen to these kids and take drastic action then? Why didn't the politicians do what needed to be done? Why?*

She read and read … and after hours and hours of reading and thinking … and reading and thinking some more - it hit her smack in the head.

She got it. She knew why all those amazing kids failed. Then all this thinking began to get to her. It began with a tightness in her lower back, then squeezed up her spine, then stung the back of her neck, then stabbed her head. She tried rotating her head to ease the pain. But it wouldn't go away. Because she knew what needed to happen next.

Chapter 7: Is honesty the best policy?

MANDALAY WAS PETRIFIED. EITHER GUTE and Jazmin were going to hate her or think she was nuts, or both. She stuffed the articles she printed into her backpack and headed down to the Hudson. She knew where Gute and Jazmin liked to swim. When she got there, she saw them way offshore, goofing around on a raft, having a jolly time in the cool water. *And why not*, she thought to herself, *it was 98 degrees - and nearing winter.* The river was crowded with swimmers. Mandalay sat under a palm tree and waited. After an hour or so they paddled in and were surprised to see their good friend sitting there, resting her back against the tree.

"Hey guys," Mandalay shouted out.

"Hey, you OK?" Gute shouted back, as they dragged their raft up the sandy beach. "You've been dodging us for a couple of days."

"Yeah, well - been doing stuff," Mandalay said, nodding.

"Want to go swimming?" Jazmin asked, smiling.

Mandalay shook her head. "No thanks. I think we need to talk."

"Is something wrong?" Jazmin asked, a little concerned.

"No," Mandalay said. "Just have something on my mind." They grabbed their towels and sat under the palm tree.

"You guys recall that crazy dude on the subway?" Mandalay asked. "Remember all that stuff he was saying about *The Big Heat?*"

"Yeah, sure. He didn't say anything I didn't already know," Jazmin said. "The world is broiling and it's a huge problem."

"Yeah, a huge problem," Gute agreed. "I read a book, *Zeitoun*, about Hurricane Katrina, from a long time ago. But now it's much worse - more hurricanes. More everything. But no one cares anymore."

"Yeah, that's the problem," Mandalay said, pausing, self-conscious. "So, uhm, I've been thinking a lot about what that guy said. He kind of shook me up. For the past week, I've been reading a lot in the library. I wasn't really sick. I'm sorry, I lied to you about that."

"So you ditched us to read about global warming?" Gute said, laughing. "I've been ditched for worse things."

"But why'd you lie about it?" Jazmin asked. "Why didn't you just tell us?"

"Well, it's complicated."

She was staring at her friends.

"Yeah, ok," Jazmin said, impatiently. "Why would you lie to us? I don't get that."

"Just please let me explain, ok? The world has a really big problem and the government and most people out there are not doing anything to stop it, right?"

"Yeah, but this is old news," Gute said. "Before we were born people were trying to stop global warming - and look how far they got."

"Fine, but we need to do something now," Mandalay said.

"What are we gonna do that hasn't been done already?" Jazmin asked. "I mean, we're ninth graders. And kids have been trying for years. Protests, marches, all that stuff."

"I know," Mandalay said. She pulled the stack of printed articles out from her backpack. "I read a lot about what happened."

She pointed at all the people swimming in the Hudson.

"That's part of the problem. Everyone has gotten used to the heat." She shook her head. "Everyone forgot what's happening: that climate change and the global warming it has caused is the biggest problem - *the biggest freakin' problem, even worse than the pandemic* - that humans have ever faced. Instead of swimming in the Hudson, we should be trying to stop global warming."

Jazmin and Gute glanced at each other before turning their attention back to Mandalay.

"Mandalay, where's all this coming from?" asked a surprised Jazmin, not understanding her friend. "If you want us to write letters to politicians, that's cool."

"Yeah, we can organize a letter writing campaign," Gute added. "I'm game for that. Or maybe start some sort of club at school to fight global warming."

Mandalay listened. She looked at her friends. She was still holding the articles in her hand.

"I lied about something else, too," Mandalay finally blurted out. "I mean, this other lie is much bigger. I love you guys, so I need to tell you. Then you'll understand everything - where I'm coming from."

"What are you talking about?" Jazmin asked, narrowing her gaze, all of a sudden wary of her friend.

"I didn't move to New York because of my dad's job."

"What?" Gute and Jazmin both said at the same time, staring at Mandalay.

Mandalay squirmed.

"I had to leave my town in Maine because I did something. I had no choice."

She hesitated as she looked at her two new friends, friends she really liked, friends she didn't want to piss off. "I got kicked out of school for doing something."

"Don't tell me you were smoking weed or something worse," Jazmin said. "Because my mom wants me to be a doctor. If she catches me hanging with the wrong kids, she'll kill me."

Mandalay shook her head. "No, no, it's not like that. I am uhm - well, I ... I can be a bit crazy sometimes."

"Yeah, you're acting a bit crazy today, that's for sure," Gute said.

"Yeah, well ..." Mandalay said, shaking her head in agreement.

"Well what?" Jazmin shot back, losing patience.

Mandalay took another deep breath, looked directly at her friends and then proceeded to tell them all about the Big Shaboozle: breaking into school, her message on the blackboard in bright red lipstick, and, of course, destroying the dweebs with a bonfire ... and that there were two Principal Bushwicks ... and Judge Baxter's threat hanging over her head like a 100-ton weight.

"Are you kidding me?" a shocked Gute shot out. "Two Bushwicks? And you did what? That's insane." He was shaking his head.

"I'm sorry. I know I should have told you," Mandalay said, looking at both her friends, feeling awfully guilty.

"No, I mean, it's amazing. What you did was amazing!" Gute half shouted.

"Yeah, how did you plan such a thing?" Jazmin asked, clearly totally impressed.

"Well, I just did," Mandalay said, shrugging, trying to hold back a proud smile. "I just planned it." She paused for a second.

"Ok, so you want to write some letters or do something at school to fight global warming - and stay out of trouble," Gute said. "Right?"

"Well, uhm, sort of," Mandalay said, only half smiling, because she was thinking a little differently. "Actually, we need to take it up a notch ... or two ... or three." She was no longer smiling.

Mandalay let those words sit there for a second, then added, "We have to do a lot more. We have to do something special."

Jazmin and Gute glanced at each other once again, not sure what she was talking about.

"What do you mean?" Jazmin asked hesitantly, not sure she wanted to hear the answer.

"We're going to have to study - really study global warming and basically become world experts," Mandalay explained, shaking her head up and down. "We're going to have to learn the facts and figures. With knowledge, we'll be taken more seriously and our demands won't look stupid."

"You know, kids tried this already and they failed," Gute said.

"I know. I read all about what they did," Mandalay said, holding up the pile of articles. "I read all about it - and I think I know why they failed." She paused for a second.

She held up that article from 2022, the one with the headline

Three Million Kids March on Washington

"That's an amazing thing," Mandalay said. "They all knew their stuff. But they failed because Washington wasn't ready - and the kids didn't do something extraordinary. Adults drove them to Washington in buses. They talked and chanted and shouted. They testified before Congress. Went on TV. They wrote articles and books and did lots of stuff. But in the end, all the kids went home ... *they went home. They left - before they got what they wanted.* Same thing in other parts of the world. Kids went home, they stopped protesting and fighting *before* they got what they wanted. That's the problem. We need to plan this on our own - and what we do needs to be extraordinary - *extraordinary*. We need to shock the world into action." Then she laughed. "We need to shock the world out of their buttholes. I mean it. I really mean it."

They all cracked up, but only for a second. Because Gute and Jazmin were looking at Mandalay with awfully hairy eyeballs, wondering what their good friend - who they now knew had some super-activist gene shooting her forward - had up her sleeve? *What in God's name was she thinking?*

Chapter 8: Here comes Gertrude

A FEW DAYS LATER, A FUNNY thing happened at the garbage bin. Tom Hawk was tossing out the garbage at the same time as neighbor Mary Johnson.

She asked about Mandalay.

Tom Hawk told her that Mandalay was a good kid, and a ninth grader with a stubborn streak and an activist's mind. He explained that just the other day, she came home from school vowing, once again, to fight global warming. He didn't tell Mary that he was holding his breath.

"Oh my, you don't say - going after global warming," Mary said, enthusiastically. She went into her apartment and returned a minute later with a scrap of paper.

"This is my baby sister Gertrude's telephone number. She can help Mandalay. She's 93 ¼, and smarter than you and I put together."

"Thank you Mary," Tom Hawk said, smiling. "I'll give her the number."

But he knew it was pointless. He knew Mandalay would never call her.

PART 3: HOT ... AND GETTING HOTTER

Chapter 1: Humans - killing everything!

G UTE AND JAZMIN AGREED TO follow Mandalay's lead. Three days later it was 99. *On December 2.*

Because of their no-tech deal with Gute, they agreed not to use any devices for reading or research, including rings, dweebs or mindmachines, the newest touch-screen computers that dangled by a steel cable from ceilings everywhere. After school, they walked to the public library. They first decided to compile a list of books, articles and reports they felt they should read.

Gute had even begun doing a little digging at home and found a quote in an old book by a famous philosopher dude from like a gazillion years ago. Gute wrote it down:

For also knowledge itself is power, by Francis Bacon

"I guess this means the more we know, the more power we'll have," Gute said.

"Yeah, it means we need to study our brains out," Mandalay added, nodding at her friends.

They printed articles and checked out a lot of books and magazines from the library.

At Mandalay's apartment, they made a lettuce, tomato, cheese and seaweed salad, marched down to Riverside Park and sat in the shade on a bench facing the Hudson River. They shared the salad, gulped ice water and read. To start, they focused on global warming's impact on animals.

"This is so sad," Jazmin said, as she held a copy of the magazine *Extinction* in her hands and read out loud. "Seals in the Arctic Sea, penguins in Antarctica, turtles in the Pacific. Oh my God –

this list is endless – possums in Australia, butterflies in Spain, the honeycreeper bird in Hawaii … They're gone or dying. We're just killing them off."

"What about the Panamanian golden frog?" Mandalay added, as she read from a book. "We've killed them off, too."

"It's not just that they're dying, but it's what this represents," Gute added, as they all read together from the famous book *The Sixth Extinction.*

In the past 450 million years on earth, a mind-boggling long period of time, there had been five so-called mass extinctions, the book explained. A mass extinction is when a significant number of living things on earth is wiped out.

The most well-known, and last, mass extinction occurred approximately 66 million years ago, when a massive asteroid struck earth, or massive volcanoes erupted, or both happened relatively close in time, scientists said, killing off the dinosaurs.

"So now, all these writers and scientists are saying we're heading towards a sixth extinction much quicker than expected, all because of man-made global warming," Jazmin explained. "And the dying frogs and all these other creatures gone missing are examples of the mess we've created."

Gute picked up a magazine called **VANISHING**.

That was the one and only word on the cover. Gute opened the magazine to a large photograph of a fluffy white polar bear sunning herself on the ice, with two sleeping cubs nestled beside her. "Matilda with cubs, Squirt and Bouncy," the caption read.

Gute turned the page to a large headline.

Gone

Gute read out loud: *"Not only are Matilda and her babies, Squirt and Bouncy, gone, but almost all the polar bears in the world are gone. In 2015, there were approximately 26,000 polar bears living in the Arctic region of the world. Today, in the year 2030, there are only about 1,000 polar bears left. By 2035, or 2040, there may be no more polar bears left in the world. None. The end of polar bears on earth is within sight."*

Gute paused to look at his friends, who were listening closely. No one was smiling.

Gute continued: *"The reason they are dying: The melting of Arctic ice due to global warming. The primary source of food for polar bears is seals. Polar bears hunt for seals from the ice. Without the ice as their perch, they lose their ability to hunt. Polar bears are starving to death. If you want to see what starving polar bears look like, please turn the page. If it is too painful to look, then don't turn the page. But take our word for it: Polar bears are close to extinction because of global warming – because people on earth have not done enough to stop it."*

Gute was staring at the article, but he did not turn the page. He took a deep breath.

"No way am I going to look at that photo. No way," he said.

Jazmin took the magazine, paused for a second and turned the page, so she could see for herself what global warming was doing to the polar bears. She stared at the photo of starving polar bears, then closed the magazine.

"Oh God, that's sad," she said, tearing up as she took a deep breath. Mandalay put a comforting hand on Jazmin's shoulder.

"Yeah, really sad," Mandalay said, also taking a noticeable breath to steady herself.

The three of them sat there silently for a few minutes, no one sure what to say, until Mandalay just spoke the truth.

"God, we are destructive, aren't we?" she said. "I don't think people really understand what's happening."

They looked out into the Hudson, watching the red-orange sunset dissolve into pale orange, then streaks of orangey-gray, before darkening to black over New Jersey.

A beautiful sight. An ugly world.

For the next three months, all they did was study. They didn't discuss strategy or a plan (because they didn't have one). They just studied. Every day after school, they lugged their heavy backpacks to the public library on Broadway and 113th Street, grabbed a table on the second floor, sat down, guzzled ice water, and read book after book, article after article.

It was clear what had happened: So many of the world's great scientists, from the United States and everywhere else, had studied and written about the devastating impact of climate change that there was no doubt that humans were causing a catastrophe, yet governments, corporations and people worldwide were not doing nearly enough to stop it.

And did they really need more proof than what they lived through every day? Winter of 2031, in reality a perpetual summer, was now called *dumberbummersummer* by scientists. That's right, summer in winter was called *dumberbummersummer*. Climatologists coined that new season because of the warmest winter mankind had ever seen. *The Big Heat* professor on the subway was right. The Indian-summer heat of fall in New York gave way to tropical 90s in winter. *Yeah, an August heat wave in January.* A lot of swimming in the Hudson. One poetic climatologist explained it this way: *"On the wings of humankind's stupidity, earth was now melting/drowning/burning/crumbling into oblivion – into dumberbummersummer."*

There was no way to know for sure if this was the new norm. But it was *dumberbummersummer* for now. *Hot!*

Sweating and stinking were so common that people had stopped using deodorant. Stink towel recycling was the hottest business in town.

The hot weather had caused a drought in America's breadbasket – where America's wheat was grown. With a shortage of wheat, there was no regular bread - *and no normal pizza.*

"God - someday - I'd like to eat a decent pepperoni pie again," Gute said, disgusted. "I'm sick of rice crust pizza, tofu muffins, seaweed wraps filled with crap - *echh.* Nothing tastes good anymore."

After all their reading, they knew that conditions in other parts of the U.S. were much worse than in New York.

There was a lot of extreme weather caused by global warming: category 5 hurricanes in the South killed 50,000 people; tornadoes were wiping out towns in the Midwest; another MaineCane trapped and killed more than 500 senior citizens in nursing homes and thousands more on the coast; monsoon-like rainblasts caused rapid flooding along the Mississippi and Missouri rivers and in major cities coast to coast - killing thousands more and causing tens of thousands to flee their homes; and severe droughts were the cause of a double whammy: they caused wildfires all across the country, hitting 29 states, leaving a constant gray haze in the air, causing breathing problems and killing thousands more ... and the same droughts were drying up lakes, rivers and reservoirs, causing 15 states to ration water. People were dying of dehydration.

"As a species, we're pathetic," Jazmin blurted out after reading article after article in the library. "We just let this happen. To satisfy the materialism of our civilization, more and more fossil fuel is still being burned to manufacture the products we all use – dweebs, mindmachines and rings and the mini-drones that are now as common as birds in the sky. It's really disgusting." She shook her head.

"Yeah," Gute added. "Refrigerators, stoves, washing machines, dryers and cars, and all the extra clothes we *must* have. Do I really need five pairs of sneakers and six pairs of jeans? *Do I?*" He shook his head in frustration.

"The truth is - we're killing ourselves," Mandalay said simply, nodding at her friends. "We're just killing ourselves. And it's all inspired by the good old U.S.A., the country that's supposed to set an example for the world."

Mandalay then picked up her pen and wrote in large, black letters in her notebook:

If humans do not go back in time, there will be no future!!!

Jazmin nodded and took the pen from Mandalay and wrote:

Only if we change now, will there be a future... WE MUST CHANGE NOW!!!

Chapter 2: New Manhattan Bay

As time moved on, they studied climate change so intensely they forgot about pretty much everything else, including their school work. They cut school one morning and took a field trip to southern Manhattan – where lawyers and stockbrokers used to work, but now fish swam in murky, green water. They wore orange rubber bodysuits, polyurethane hoodies and huge, floppy sunhats on yet another broiling day.

They took the #1 subway south to Rector Street. The train used to go further south to Bowling Green, but that was before the flooding and before the Hudson and East rivers merged to form New Manhattan Bay. Mandalay, Gute and Jazmin exited the station and walked a block south. A large metal sign said:

Entrance is FORBIDDEN and ILLEGAL.
Risk of drowning due to riptide.

They climbed over the blue police barriers and then clipped the barbed wire with wire cutters. It was a scene out of an end-of-the-world movie: Empty buildings, rusted cars and flood waters lapping against the sides of buildings. Six years earlier, lower Broadway was a noisy and bustling hub in New York City, filled with office workers, tourists, cars, buses and taxis. Now, the streets were drop-dead quiet and were covered with two feet of stinky, yucky, greenish water and no people. Garbage was rotting in the water, as small fish and crab swam about. The Bowling Green subway station was now, officially, part of New Manhattan Bay, like a sunken ship from centuries ago. Water Street, finally, was appropriately named, because it was under water.

"This is a little scary," Mandalay said to her friends, as they waded around the abandoned streets – streets that now looked like the flooded ones in southern Louisiana or coastal Florida. They entered an abandoned seafood restaurant with no door, but only found fish swimming through the shallow water in the kitchen.

"This is a bit of revenge," Gute said. "They won't be frying these guys anymore."

They waded through Battery Park at the very tip of Manhattan, the tourists replaced by the gentle waves of New Manhattan Bay. The Statue of Liberty was off in the distance, the bottom third underwater.

"The president of the United States and every politician in Washington should pay a visit," Jazmin said. "How can they possibly say climate change isn't destroying us?"

Well, it turned out this little field trip would create a big problem for Mandalay, Gute and Jazmin. They had forgotten to call school and give a phony excuse about their absence.

"I thought you called," Mandalay said to Jazmin. And Jazmin said to Mandalay, "I thought you did."

Principal Bushwick had not thought much about Mandalay, Gute and Jazmin in many months. He was informed of their unexcused absence. He was suspicious that he had not heard anything about them in months, so he did a little digging. What he learned made him angry - *really angry*. He wrote three letters.

Dear Mr. Hawk:

I am writing to inform you that your daughter cut school today and is close to failing math, science, history, English and Spanish. In the past month, she has received Fs on all tests in all five subjects. Cutting school and flunking grades are unacceptable. It appears to me as if your child has just stopped trying in school.

I need to remind you that all students at Ernest Hemingway

High School must come to school and maintain passing grades.
If Mandalay continues to get Fs, she will flunk out of school.

Yours truly,
Principal Homer Bushwick

PS: As you know, Judge Baxter will be informed if your
daughter flunks out.

He wrote a similar letter to Gute's dad and Jazmin's mom, minus the PS.

A few days later, when Mandalay got home, her dad was sitting on the couch. Mandalay knew something was wrong right away, because her dad did not say hello. He just kind of cleared his throat when she entered, the guttural parental warning indicating he was upset about something she did.

"Hey dad," Mandalay said hesitantly, noticing a letter on the table.

"Sweetheart, we need to talk," her dad said flatly, sounding too much like a tough-love dad.

Mandalay placed her backpack on the floor and walked over.

"I got this letter today from Principal Bushwick."

He handed Mandalay the letter. She read it.

"The first thing is - I didn't know your principal was named Bushwick. Second, I didn't know he knew about Judge Baxter. Want to explain?"

Mandalay's dad looked angry, perhaps as angry when she told him about the Big Shaboozle.

"Well, dad ..." she began, nervously. "You see, uhm ..."

Her dad interrupted. "Sweetheart, just tell me the whole story - ok."

Mandalay took a breath. "Ok, ok," she said. And then she proceeded to tell him the entire, unbelievable story about the two Bushwicks ... and how the one in Maine told the one in New York about Judge Baxter.

Tom Hawk was shaking his head. "That's unbelievable. Why didn't you tell me?" he asked.

"Because I didn't want to worry you dad. I didn't mean ..."

"You should have told me," he interrupted again, this time even angrier. "You should have told me. And you need to start studying. You can't flunk out of school."

He was staring at his daughter.

"Dad, you know we're studying global warming. That's all we do," Mandalay said. "It's the most important ..."

He interrupted her again: "It's not the most important thing. You can't flunk out of school. If you do, Judge Baxter will ship you off to you know where. And I don't want that to happen."

Mandalay shook her head. "Bushwick's a creep. He's just a big fat creep," she said angrily.

"Yeah, he may be a creep," Tom Hawk said, "but he's the principal of your school, and if you cut class and fail all your tests, he'll throw you out."

Mandalay began shaking her head, shaking it in anger.

"Dad, why aren't you on my side? *Why!?!* We visited the flood zone in lower Manhattan. There are fish swimming where people used to live and work! And are you forgetting what happened in Maine? That freakin' MaineCane almost killed me!"

She let those angry words sink in. She took a deep, frustrated breath, then added, "We're working so hard to study and make a difference - why aren't you supporting me?"

"Darling, I want to give you the freedom to follow your conscience, I do." He nodded with half a smile as he gently placed his hand on Mandalay's shoulder. But after a moment, his gaze hardened and his jaw tensed. "But I also know what will happen if you get in trouble."

Mandalay shook her head and looked away. She got up from the couch, went into the kitchen and grabbed some leftovers.

"What my friends and I are doing is far more important than studying in school," she said, as she stormed off to her room. "If I get thrown out of school, who gives a crap."

As for Jazmin's mom, she was so pissed off, she said only one thing to her daughter: "You better fix this. That's all I know. You better fix this." Then she handed the letter to Jazmin.

Gute got off easy because he intercepted the letter. That can happen when your dad has a job that keeps him working late. Gute read the letter, knew he was failing, but did not expect such a dark warning from the principal.

"Shoot," was all Gute said to himself, as he tore up the letter and flushed it down the toilet.

Chapter 3: Nap time

STRANGE, REALLY STRANGE, HOW SOMETIMES things work out. It was the next day at Hemingway High, the first class in fact.

History was taught by Mr. Harkness. Some students called him Ancient H, because, at age 78, he was the oldest teacher in the school – *by far*. Sometimes, he would say in a very serious tone, "The reason I know so much about history is because I lived through it."

In class that day, Mandalay had her textbook open and her global warming notes tucked inside the book (for studying), but she was having trouble staying awake. She was exhausted. She hadn't slept much the night before because she was angry at her dad and stayed up late studying you know what. She kept nodding off. This kept happening, until she just gave in. She put her elbows on her desk, rested her head on her hands, closed her eyes, relaxed, and fell fast asleep.

"After the Great Depression," Mr. Harkness explained to the class, "we have learned that the government began the New Deal. This was a program to create large public works projects and jobs for millions of unemployed people. When was the next turning point in U.S. history?"

Lots of hands shot up. Mr. Harkness pointed to a girl in the back.

"The Japanese bombed Pearl Harbor on December 7, 1941. President Roosevelt called it 'A date which will live in infamy,' " said Rebecca Tolstoy, known as the smartest kid in the class. "The U.S. joined World War II soon after. This was Japan's and Germany's worst nightmare."

"Very good, Rebecca," Mr. Harkness said. "So class, when the U.S. entered the war, was it prepared to fight? Remember, the country was just coming out of the Depression."

Several hands shot up, but Mr. Harkness noticed Mandalay, in the back, her head resting peacefully on her hands, eyes shut, snoozing away.

Mr. Harkness walked towards Mandalay. The class could see this coming. So could Gute and Jazmin, who began to cringe at the thought of what was about to happen.

Mr. Harkness slowly walked up to Mandalay, bent over slightly in her direction, clasped his hands behind his back, smiled an insincere, sour-puss smile, and shouted: *Mandalay Hawk!*"

Mandalay was so startled she jolted upright, sending her textbook and notes flying off her desk.

Several kids laughed, then muffled themselves.

"Ms. Hawk, I'm very sorry to disturb your sleep, but this is not kindergarten nap time. This is high school history class," Mr. Harkness said angrily.

"The question is, in 1941, after the Japanese bombed Pearl Harbor, was the U.S. prepared for World War II? Was it, Ms. Hawk?" Mr. Harkness asked, as he glared down at her.

"Well," Mandalay began, still trying to wake up as she rubbed her eyes.

Mr. Harkness shook his head. Hands shot up as he turned towards the class.

"Remember, that class participation counts for one quarter of your grade," he said, then added, as he turned back towards Mandalay, "but if you fail all your tests, it doesn't really matter if you participate or not."

He pointed to another student. "Yes, Charlie."

"What happened is that …" Charlie Scott began, but before he could say another word, Mandalay interrupted.

"Actually, it was 1940. May 1940 to be precise, when an extraordinary event occurred regarding U.S. history and its preparation for war," Mandalay said, standing up, because she had a lot to say.

Mr. Harkness and the entire class looked at her in surprise.

"1940? My dear girl, the Japanese bombed Pearl Harbor on December 7, 1941," Mr. Harkness reminded her. "Everyone knows that."

"Yes, I'm aware of that date," Mandalay explained. "But something very important to the U.S. war effort happened before Japan bombed Pearl Harbor."

"And what might that be?" Harkness asked, expecting Mandalay to fall flat on her face in front of the entire class.

"That was when President Roosevelt took action," Mandalay said. "By May 1940, Germany had already started its path towards World War II. Roosevelt knew a war was coming. He didn't wait for Pearl Harbor to start planning."

Gute and Jazmin glanced at each other, wondering the same thing: *Wasn't Mandalay supposed to be studying global warming?*

"The key date was May 28, 1940. Roosevelt made a single phone call, to Mr. Bill Knudsen, the president of General Motors. GM manufactured automobiles – it made the most in the world. This would be like calling the president of Ring-a-Ling Phones or DweebCentral today. Bill Knudsen was the industrial genius of his time. Roosevelt asked him to quit his job and move to Washington to be in charge of U.S. war production. The U.S. did not have enough planes, ships, guns, bullets, tanks or really enough of anything to fight Germany and Japan.

"So what did Bill Knudsen do?" Mandalay asked rhetorically, pausing to take a confident breath, sounding more like a college professor than a ninth grader. "He did exactly what the president asked him to do. He quit his job and moved to Washington. He convinced the auto industry to stop making cars and start making planes, tanks, guns and bullets for the war. The U.S. ended up manufacturing 300,000 warplanes and more than 100,000 ships.

"We won the war, in part, because we built more planes, more ships and more guns than our enemies. It all began with a phone call to Bill Knudsen."

Mandalay Hawk nodded and then sat down. Mr. Harkness wasn't quite sure what to say or do. He had been upstaged by a sleeping, flunking student.

"I see, well, yes, very interesting," was all he could say. He knew nothing about Knudsen, little about the U.S. war effort before 1941, so he could not dispute what Mandalay had said.

Chapter 4: From bad to worse, then...

AFTER SCHOOL, MR. HARKNESS SUMMONED Mandalay, Gute and Jazmin to his classroom. This could not be good. They looked at each other, knowing full well they had solid F averages, with Bushwick's letter a constant threat.

"I've been teaching for a long time, 54 years to be exact. You're flunking *and* sleeping in my class. You don't care. And then today we had Mandalay's show and tell."

He held up a letter. "I plan to submit this to Principal Bushwick."

Gute took a deep breath. Jazmin began to shake her head. Mandalay held up her hands.

They assumed they were getting the boot. "But Mr. Harkness," Mandalay said. "We ..."

He interrupted her. "This is my last day at Hemingway High. I'm resigning. I wanted the three of you to know first."

"What?" was all a stunned Mandalay could say.

"Today must have been a practical joke. I'm sure the whole class was in on it," he said. "I was humiliated. I was embarrassed. I must be totally out of touch."

"Mr. Harkness, no," Mandalay said, shaking her head. "We were not playing a joke."

"You don't have to hide it. I'm an old, crusty dinosaur. Time for me to move on."

"No," Gute said, as the three of them shook their heads at the same time.

"It's true, we can't stay awake, but it has nothing to do with your teaching," explained Jazmin, sympathetically, who also had nodded off a few times. "You're a good teacher."

"Then what's going on?" Mr. Harkness asked impatiently.

They sat down and explained the whole story. Mandalay said she had been studying America's preparation for World War II because it would help her understand how the U.S. could take extreme action quickly to defeat global warming. She added: "And because of all our studying, we don't get much sleep."

Mr. Harkness had listened. Then he just sat there thinking. He looked at the floor. He looked up. He took a deep breath.

"You don't say," he finally said. "Is all that really true?"

"Yes," the three of them said at the same time.

Mr. Harkeness nodded.

"Gosh, you crazy, foolish kids," he said smiling, chuckling softly. "Kids have been trying for years to fight global warming. A lot of action, not much results. And politicians - they're either clueless, spineless or just don't do enough." He shook his head. "What you're trying to do is about the toughest thing in the world, that's for sure. But at least you're trying. Gotta give you credit."

He thought for a moment.

"You know, when I was in high school, a long, long time ago, I cut a few days of school to march against the Vietnam War. I almost got expelled. My parents wanted to kill me. But you know what, those were some of the most inspiring days of my life."

He picked up the envelope with his letter of resignation and slapped it against his other hand. "That's right. One of the best things I ever did – because I stood up for what I believed in."

Then he pursed his lips, nodded his head up and down and ripped the envelope in half. "Ok, I'm not resigning. But you know what, sleeping in my class isn't the answer. You won't need to do that again."

Chapter 5: Better study your brains out, or else!

T HE NEXT DAY IN MATH class, Mandalay, Gute and Jazmin each did their usual thing: back row, climate change material stuck inside their math book, so that they could keep studying. It was either that, or take a nap, which, they now knew, could backfire big time.

The moment the bell rang: "Mandalay, Gute and Jazmin, I need to speak with you," Ms. Jenkins, the math teacher, said sternly. They all thought of Mr. Harkness – about how he must have turned on them and ratted them out.

When they saw Mr. Harkness in the hallway before class, he turned his head in the other direction, as if they had some dreaded, contagious disease, and kept walking.

"Sit down, please," Ms. Jenkins said. "I know what's going on." She held up a copy of Bushwick's letter. "You shouldn't be thrown out of school because you're trying to save the world." She said those words with a straight face.

Then she ripped up the letter from Bushwick.

"I've talked to Harkness. I understand what you're trying to do. I don't want to be too pessimistic, so I'll just say *good luck*. Because you're gonna need it. You're now on independent study for the rest of the year. Your only assignment: study climate change and its impact. But you have to promise me: You'll study your brains out - got it?"

Then, the same thing happened at the end of science, English and Spanish class: Independent study, with instructions to study really hard. At the end of history class, Mr. Harkness said, simply:

"I don't want to see you again in my classroom. Go to the library. A room has been reserved for you."

Mandalay, Gute and Jazmin were so stunned they didn't know what to say. Until Jazmin finally asked, "Are you sure? How are we gonna get away with this?"

Mr. Harkness looked down, then out the window. Then he walked over to the classroom door and closed it. He then faced the three kids standing in front of him. "I've been teaching at this school for a long time. Bushwick may be principal, but I know everyone at this school. *Everyone.* They trust me. They believe in me. When I tell you something, you can rest assured it will get done. And climate change is the biggest problem the world has ever faced. So I commend you for what you're doing. You'll almost certainly fail ... but fighting it is far more important than coming to school every day and doing your school work." He nodded.

Then he walked over to his desk and picked up his briefcase. He went to the door, opened it and walked out.

Chapter 6: Climate refugees - from Florida!

T HEY HAD THE GREEN LIGHT to do what needed to be done. They studied their brains out, in and out of school, every day, reading, taking notes, discussing the issues. Mandalay turned 14, but she ignored her birthday and kept on studying.

They read about the droughts, the floods, the sea rise, the food shortages, the water rationing, the wildfires and the refugee problem. And they took more local field trips, because the impact of global warming was right in front of them.

After school one day, they walked down to the northern section of Riverside Park, along the Hudson River. As they approached, they could smell the food being cooked on campfires. What they found in the park were thousands and thousands of people living in hundreds of large blue government tents, stretching for blocks, in what was now called *New South Village*. Old people, young people, families with kids and their dogs, living outdoors in the baking sun. They cooked food over open fires. Hundreds of portable toilets lined the walkway. These were climate refugees, who had fled Florida, Louisiana and Mississippi because of the floods and sea rise and had come to New York for a new life. Mandalay, Gute and Jazmin went there to talk to them.

"We could have stayed in Key West and lived on our boat," said Lotus Davenport, a young woman with long brown hair, talking about a lost island of Florida. "But there was no place to buy food, because the Atlantic Ocean just rose and rose right into our grocery store. The health clinic, the school - all gone, too. We got our family photos and clothes and, of course, Romper and we took a bus here."

Sitting by her side on the grass, head lying on top of his paws, was Romper, a shaggy golden retriever, who knew no better. Neither did her two young boys, lying in the tent, fast asleep.

Then it was Walter Bell's turn. "You know how the water in a bathtub rises ever so slowly if the water is dripping? Well, that's what happened to us," explained Bell, about 60, from Plaquemines Parish, Louisiana, with brown, sun-leathered skin, a soft smile curling his lips. "We knew it was coming, sure did, but slowly. We lived just down the road from the coast, in a house my grandfather built." He took a puff on his cigarette and blew smoke away from them.

"We had hurricanes and stuff and dealt with the high water. But those times, the water always left. But not now. The distance between our house and the bay just kept shrinking. And then that murky brown water just kept coming up towards our front door, inch by inch. Kept coming. We put down some old shingles and sandbags – tried to make a little dam - but that was the dumbest thing we ever did. How are sandbags gonna stop the bay from gettin' into your house if it wants to? You want to tell me - huh? Then one morning, drip, drip, shuggle, shuggle … like the tide coming in. Except the tide never went back out. We lived for a month with that smelly water in our living room."

He shook his head, then smiled again. "Nah, we couldn't keep doing that. Nah." He was shaking his head. "Bus brought us here." He took another puff on his cigarette and blew the smoke into the air, which carried with the light breeze. His wife sat nearby on a folding chair, staring out into the Hudson. "We got nothing left," he said. He wasn't smiling anymore.

As they walked through *New South Village* and saw all the kids, filthy from living outside, Mandalay, Gute and Jazmin took quick glances at each other and shook their heads. There wasn't much they could say. There were now climate refugee villages like this all over the country. They knew, after what they had just heard and after months of studying, their time for action was fast approaching.

Chapter 7: Meeting Gertrude Johnson under a palm tree

THEY AGREED NOT TO TELL their parents what they planned. But it was as if Mandalay's dad, somehow, knew he was being deceived. He felt he had to assert some control over his daughter - a little tough love - because he was perpetually afraid she would get in trouble.

He told her about the talk he had with the neighbor, Mary Johnson, which explained the note Mandalay got in the mail from Gertrude Johnson. Gertrude said she "knew someone who knew someone who knew someone."

"I have no idea what that means, dad," Mandalay said in frustration. "And I don't even know this lady."

"So what. Maybe she can help you," he said. "And it's only a little … whatever. I want you to meet her, please."

Mandalay Shmoogled Gertrude Johnson and turned up this: 93 years old with a triple PhD in earth science, atmospheric physics and meteorological climatology from Stanford and had been a Columbia professor for 45 years.

The note said to meet her on Saturday, at 11 am, on the western most bench on the north side of the Grand Canal, "under that HUGE palm tree."

When Mandalay arrived, she found a little old lady wearing a simple navy blue dress and a large straw sunhat sitting on the bench.

"You must be Mandalay," Gertrude Johnson said in a sweet, soft voice, smiling and holding out her hand.

"Yes, that's me," Mandalay said, sticking out her hand. Gertrude took it with both hands and clasped it warmly. "Dearie, it's so nice to meet you."

Mandalay smiled. *She was a nice old lady, so maybe this won't be too bad*, Mandalay began thinking.

"I brought you a piece of my special butter cake, sweetheart, I hope you like it."

She opened a tin with two pieces of cake. Mandalay sat down next to her.

"Please help yourself," Gertrude said, "and then please tell me how you and your friends plan on saving the world."

Nothing embarrasses a kid more than having their own words or actions shoved right back in their face.

Mandalay blushed and took a big bite, so she didn't have to respond right away.

"Take your time, dearie, but we're not leaving here until you tell me every single detail," Gertrude said, smiling, but clearly no nonsense. "Tell me the story, from the beginning."

Mandalay swallowed and then took a deep breath. "Okay," she said, and then she proceeded to tell Gertrude the whole shebang, how they all had their heads in the sand for so long, and how, when dumberbummersummer came to town, with a wake up call from Professor *Big Heat*, they realized there was a problem that needed their attention. *Now.*

"We have studied this issue like crazy. Now, we're planning an encounter in New York City, with about 100,000 kids, telling the mayor and the governor what needs to be done. They'll have to listen. They'll have no choice. Because this is not a rally - this is an *encounter*. The first of many."

Mandalay liked to think big – but an *encounter* with *100,000 kids? The first of many? What the heck was that about?* Well, she just made that whole thing up - just spit it out. She had not talked about it with Gute or Jazmin. But it didn't matter.

Because Gertrude liked to think big, too. In fact, Gertrude Johnson lived for thinking big.

"Well, when you have your *encounter* in Washington, you'll need my help, that's for sure," Gertrude said, matter of factly.

Mandalay nodded, even though she had no idea what Gertrude was talking about, because Washington was awfully far away. Gertrude wiped her mouth with her napkin, closed the metal tin and placed it in her bag. She smiled at Mandalay. "You'll be hearing from me, dearie. Keep on studying." She nodded and walked off.

Chapter 8: Gertrude goes to work

WHEN SHE GOT HOME, GERTRUDE JOHNSON picked up the phone and dialed.

"Hello, Nettie," Gertrude said into the phone, "how's my sweet daughter doing today?"

"I'm fine, mom. How are you?"

"Well, dear, I'm fine, too. I just had the most interesting, well, extraordinary chat with a nice young lady. I need to speak with Billy. Is he home?"

"Mom, it's Sunday. Billy's at work – you know he works weekends."

Billy was Gertrude's one and only grandson. She adored him more than anyone on earth.

"Oh, yes, pardon me for having a senior moment. Well, I'm home now, and I need to speak with Billy ASAP. Would you please have him call me within the next 10 minutes."

"Mom, I love you and so does Billy. But he's working now. He'll call you tonight."

"Well, I need to speak to him now."

"Mom, you know what he does for a living, although he probably shouldn't have told you. He can't just pick up the phone and call you."

"Yeah, but sweetie, this is your mother speaking. Billy certainly must take a pee break every once in a while. Just tell him granny needs to speak with him. I love you, darling."

Gertrude hung up.

She knew it would take Billy a few minutes to get to the bathroom before calling. She decided to boil water for tea. While she did, she recalled holding Billy wrapped in a blankie when he was a baby, those sparkling blue eyes and little dimples. She had always adored and pampered Billy. And Billy always listened to granny, because, well, almost everyone listened to Gertrude Johnson, whether she was your granny or not. She just had that way about her.

By the time Gertrude had poured her tea, the phone rang.

"Hello dearie," Gertrude said.

"Hi, granny," Billy said into his ring phone, in not the happiest of voices.

"How are you, sweetheart?" she said.

"I'm good, granny. You know that I'm working, don't you?" he said.

"I know, dearie, I know. I hope you're having a great day."

"Well, granny, it's a pretty good day so far," Billy said, feeling the smallest of knots forming in his belly. He loved his granny as much as anyone in the world, but sometimes ...

"Billy, I need you to do granny a little favor."

Jeez, Billy hated those words. There was no such thing as a little favor with the job Billy had. He took a deep, nervous breath. He glanced at his watch. He needed to get back to work.

"The reason I'm calling, Billy ..."

Billy listened. He stared into the mirror. He closed his eyes for a second and shook his head. He took an even deeper breath than before.

After a few minutes of listening, Billy said, "But granny."

"Dearie, as you know, there are no buts. I love you, Billy, more than butter cake." Then she hung up.

Oh brother, Billy thought, *the butter cake line*. When Billy saw granny, she would hug him and kiss him a thousand times and when they parted, she would always say, "I love you more than butter cake."

In the end, Billy always did what granny asked. *Always*. He just had to figure out how to do it. And not get caught.

Chapter 9: Gutenberg rules!

I T HIT 95 DEGREES FOR the 9th day in a row. Mandalay, Gute and Jazmin had no appetite, so they walked in Central Park and drank ice water for lunch. Gute's stink towel was so disgusting and smelly he used the bottom of his t-shirt to wipe the sweat off his face.

They had been studying forever. Gertrude was a sharp needle in Mandalay's side - got her thinking it was time. Mandalay talked with Gute and Jazmin about holding an *encounter* at city hall on April 6 - two weeks away.

"What's an encounter?" Gute asked.

"Hm, not sure. It's kind of like ...." Mandalay said, her voice trailing off. "Kind of ... Well, not sure. But it doesn't matter. Because sometimes you just have to wing it."

Jazmin said: "We're going to have to start using our rings again and send a zapattack. It's the only way to get the word out."

She took her ring out of her pocket and put it on, to make her point.

Mandalay knew a zapattack was controversial.

"I know everyone hates those things, but desperate times does call for desperate action. Gute, are you on board?" Mandalay asked.

A zapattack meant sending a special zap, which automatically invaded the recipient's ring contact list and then forwarded the zap to everyone on the list.

"We need to reach thousands of people quickly, Gute. It's the only way," Mandalay urged.

Gute had stopped walking and put his hands in his pockets. He shook his head. "It's definitely not the only way." He shook his head some more. "And we had a deal. No tech. And a deal's a deal, unless there's an emergency and there's no other way. But there is another way. After school, we're going to my house. I need to show you something."

After the bell rang at three, they first went to the deli and bought seaweed chips and Gatorade. Then they walked the 10 blocks to Gute's apartment. When they got there, they walked into the living room, then down a long hallway to his bedroom. Gute pushed open his bedroom door, flicked on the light and said simply, "*Voila.*"

Smack in the middle of his room, taking up more space than his bed, sat a huge, metal ... *thing.*

"Meet beautiful Big Bertha," he said proudly, as if he was showing them the cutest puppy the world had ever seen.

Mandalay and Jazmin just stared, then said, at the *exact* same time: "Wow. What is it?" They did not know what else to say. It was large. It was metal. And it was very, very, *very* old.

Gute was beaming.

"This" – pointing to Bertha – "is what makes the world go round. Without this, we wouldn't have books. I've been dying to show you this for months. It's an old-time printing press. Remember, how I got my nickname - from Gutenberg. Well, he invented this thing. And without it, we'd all be in big trouble."

Gute was not using past tense, not giving an inch to modern technology, ignoring the fact that 95 percent of people under age 50 in the year 2031 hardly read anything on paper.

Gute's printing press was not even electric. Not even close to modern.

Mandalay's mind was spinning, as she tried to understand.

"This looks ... uhm, well ... *interesting*," Mandalay finally said, struggling for words. "Does it work or is it just here for ...?" She hunched her shoulders, failing to finish her sentence.

Gute laughed. "Oh yeah, it works. My dad bought it for me. Let me show you."

Mandalay and Jazmin kind of wanted to roll their eyes at

their good friend, but out of respect they did not. They watched and listened.

"Bertha makes you appreciate every word, every sentence you write, because" – pointing to the wooden box of metal letters – "it's a huge effort to print just one page."

"And remember, we had a deal." He stared at his friends, waiting. They looked at each other.

"How do we expect to reach a lot of people? I mean, this is 2031, not 1831," Mandalay said, wondering, only half kidding.

"We have to adapt. We want to stop global warming. Change is a big part of it. Plus, this machine does beautiful work." He pet it like it was his puppy.

Mandalay looked at Jazmin, shook her head again, sighed and then took her ring off and put it back in her pocket. Jazmin did the same thing.

"Thanks guys," Gute said. "Now let me show you how Bertha baby works."

He picked out a few letters and placed them in a line on a large wooden frame, to form a word. Then together they picked more letters and formed more words, setting the type. They had a sentence, then more words and another sentence. The frame was placed on the press. It took two hours for them to set the type for their flier:

KRAAP!!!
(Kids Revolt Against Adult Power)

Sun, Wind and Water Power,
or We All Die!

This heat is killing us. It's called Global Warming. It must be stopped. NOW!!!

KRAAP Encounter: Sunday, April 6, 2031, at 11 am

**We will SURROUND City Hall, NYC – just north
of New Manhattan Bay - and encircle those very
politicians and adults who got us into this mess,
trap them, and not leave until they agree
to our demands. KRAAP!!!**

They pulled the lever and over the next few days, printed hundreds of fliers and meant what they said: ***KRAAP, KRAAP, KRAAP!!!***

They were revolting against adults because they had no choice.

"I can't believe adults have allowed this to happen," Mandalay said, as they walked near Yankee Stadium in the Bronx later in the week, exhausted from the heat and lack of sleep as they handed out fliers.

"If you don't come to this encounter, this day will be a chilly memory compared to what's coming," Gute said to one kid. It was 99 degrees at 4:30 pm on this late March day.

They sweated so much walking in the heat passing out fliers that together they lost 11 pounds in a week.

A few days later, back in the Bronx, they came upon something they had hoped to avoid. It was a wood sign with carved animals on the border. The sign said:

**We mourn the loss of 59
beautiful animals, who lost their lives
on July 29, 2030**

They all knew what had happened, but this was one thing they had not wanted to talk about. It was just too sad, even worse than the polar bears, because it was so close to home. Last summer, when the average temperature was 102, and there had been no rain for a month, the wind picked up one day, causing a *sudden* forest fire that swept through the woods and into a small section of the Bronx. Miraculously, no people were killed. But the fire hit the Bronx Zoo, one of the world's most famous zoos. Zoo keepers tried to save as many animals as possible, but, in the end, the decision came down to saving humans over animals.

"I remember reading about that on the net. I was still in Maine," Mandalay said, speaking softly, solemnly, looking out at a huge pile of memorial flowers, now wilted, on the ground in front of the charred remains of the elephant and monkey houses, which remained boarded up and abandoned.

"I remember what I was doing when I heard about that, I just started crying," Jazmin said.

"Yeah," was all Gute could say, patting Jazmin on the back. "At least no people got killed."

They glanced at each other, too sad to say anything else. They walked for a while in silence, not handing out fliers ... thinking about what they had just seen, thinking about this whole mess.

"There was just one little sign where all those animals used to be," Gute finally said, shaking his head. "So now we're all just posting signs and moving on - like nothing happened."

Not that they needed more motivation, but visiting that horrible scene gave them an extra jolt. That night, they printed more fliers and pushed forward with the studying, trying to understand as best they could how the carbon emissions were permanently ruining the only habitable planet known to mankind.

Chapter 10: Will Billy end up in the slammer because of grandma?

BILLY LOVED HIS GRANDMOTHER AND always did what she asked. However, he always had to check, to make sure that what she was asking him to do would not put anyone in danger.

Late one night, he sat at his desk in his room, his door closed, his shades down (because he never knew who was watching him) and logged on to his mindmachine. *His government mindmachine.* He did a global search for Mandalay Hawk on all the private and government databases he had access to. He read about her dweeb bonfire, her lipstick message, and all the trouble she got into.

Billy took a breath. In the past year, Granny had asked for an autographed picture and there was that personal visit he arranged. But that was harmless. She had never asked for something like this before – a request that would be a major breach of security - involving a juvenile delinquent who committed a bunch of felonies in the middle of the night not too long ago.

And what about that legal oath Billy took when he was hired by the federal government? *What about that oath?* Billy thought, and wondered … and wondered some more.

"Jeez granny," he said to himself softly, shaking his head, wishing granny had never called him on this one. Because he could never say no to granny.

Chapter 11: The punk journalist

Mandalay lured Jonny Jackson to lunch by saying, "I'm telling you, this will be the story of a lifetime. I promise you."

When Jonny Jackson heard those words in the first and second phone calls, she blew Mandalay off. When Mandalay persisted with a third call, Jonny finally thought: *Well, ok, what do I have to lose?*

Jonny worked at *The Sunny Day News,* New York City's largest newspaper. She agreed to meet Mandalay, Gute and Jazmin at a diner on Broadway.

Mandalay was happy she would be turning a woman onto the story of the century, but when they first met, Mandalay wondered if it was a good idea to turn this story over to a kid. Jonny looked about 16.

They said hello, exchanged pleasantries, and then there were a few moments of awkward silence. They ordered milk shakes. When they came, Jonny couldn't control herself. She slurped down her chocolate shake so loudly she looked and sounded like a 10-year old.

"So how long have you been a reporter at *The Sunny Day News?*" Mandalay asked warily, afraid to interrupt her slurping and hear the answer.

Jonny pulled back from her straw. "Well, let me think," she said, puckering her chocolatey lips in thought. "Hmm - 19 days and counting. And by the way, I'm not technically a reporter. I'm what they call an RIT, a reporter in training. You know, I just graduated college."

Jonny had a huge smile on her face and Mandalay had a huge hole in her stomach.

"Really?" Mandalay said, definitely not smiling, wondering now even more if she had called the wrong journalist. Mandalay had called Jonny because she read a short science story in the newspaper online that Jonny had written and figured why not. *But a reporter in training?*

"And one of my first assignments: They stuck me on the science desk and I know practically nothing about science," Jonny continued with a shrug, making her case even worse.

Then she resumed slurping her shake.

Mandalay glanced at Gute and Jazmin, trying to figure out how to wiggle out of this one.

"So, uhm, perhaps …" Mandalay stammered. "I was wondering …"

Suddenly, Jonny stopped slurping, lifted her head from her straw and interrupted Mandalay.

"Perhaps I should tell you what I've written, so you can decide if you want to hand this huge story to a punk reporter like me – is that what you want to know?" Jonny asked, all of a sudden sounding tougher, wiser and more self-assured than before, as she wiped chocolate shake from her mouth with a napkin. She nodded and didn't wait for an answer.

"Three men in Chicago are free, out of prison, because of stories I wrote while a student at Northwestern University. You see, in Chicago, like in many parts of the country, we still have a lot of racism in our legal system. These three men I wrote about are black. A mostly all-white jury convicted them of murder. But the witnesses who said they did it were lying to get out of prison. And one of the men who, quote 'confessed,' to this murder" – she made quote marks with her fingers – "well, who wouldn't confess if questioned by police for 36 straight hours? I interviewed more than 100 people who live in the neighborhood where the killing took place. And you know what: the three men who were convicted of this crime and who spent 15 years in prison didn't do it. They locked up the wrong guys and the real killers got away."

Jonny was no longer smiling and didn't sound like a reporter in training.

"I see," Mandalay said, a little more confident in this reporter now.

"So what do you have for me?" Jonny asked, as she opened her reporter's notebook.

Mandalay leaned in, and so did Jazmin and Gute, and they proceeded to tell Jonny what they were about to do. Jonny wrote everything down. Page after page of notes.

And when they were done talking, Jonny looked at them and said simply: "So, you actually expect all these kids to show up and all these important people to listen and for them to make changes, just like that? Scientists have been hollering about global warming for decades. And kids have already done the protest thing. No one seems to care much about droughts, floods and all those climate immigrants. It's so common now. And everyone's gotten used to the heat."

"I thought you didn't know anything about science and stuff," a surprised Mandalay said.

"I have a basic knowledge about the impact of climate change, and I have a keen sense about unrealistic expectations."

She paused for effect.

"If I go to my editor with this story, he'll say: 'Jonny, I warned you about finding me real stories, didn't I? No one cares about global warming. It's old stuff. Our readers are tired of hearing about it. Go find me a real story.' Then he'll turn and walk away. That's what editors do. Like it's a Hollywood movie, or something."

Jonny had put down her pen and closed her notebook. Mandalay, Gute and Jazmin saw she was done taking notes, as in done taking them seriously.

"What if you don't tell your editor? What if you tag along and see for yourself that we mean business?" asked Gute. "And when you realize we're serious, then you write something."

Jonny admired determination. She liked people who were bold, especially when they were 14 years old. "I just don't want to waste my time," she said. "Because I'm a reporter in training for only 10 weeks. Then the paper decides whether I become a staff reporter. I screw up now, I'm out the door." She zipped her bag.

"We'll see," she said, then nodded, got up and walked off.

Chapter 12: Mandalay
gets serious with dad

MANDALAY GOT UP EARLY THE next day and went online to see if Jonny had written anything about them. She scanned *The Sunny Day News* website on her dad's mindmachine, looking for something about their plan to shake the powers that be. She clicked through the stories. Nothing. *Not a word.*

"Shart," a frustrated Mandalay said softly, mostly to herself.

"What did you say, darling?" her dad asked, alarmed.

"Dad, come on, give me a break," a frustrated Mandalay shot back. "I said *shart* – S-H-A-R-T. And remember, I'm a teenager, not a kid."

Mandalay had gone from a motor mouth - a kid who would tell her dad almost anything in years past - to a frustrated and intense 14-year-old with a save-the-world project, who had clammed up, shut her trap, because her dad was showing way too much tough love.

Then to top it off, her dad just blurted out: "Mandalay, you do have to plan the details. This is not some fantastic novel or movie, where Harry Potter waves a magic wand and saves the planet."

He said this because he sensed, even though Mandalay had not spelled it out, that Mandalay and her buds were nearing some kind of event - *something* - without a clue or a plan. They had not thought about obtaining a permit to hold a rally. Not planned any of the details for a large gathering, such as a loudspeaker system or portable toilets.

"What if a kid has to go to the bathroom?" Tom Hawk finally blurted out in frustration.

"Dad!" Mandalay shot back with her own frustration.

She shook her head and took a deep, noticeable, angry breath.

"Dad, you know, I love you so much. I hate it when we argue or fight. But I just have to do what I have to do."

Mandalay paused and moved closer to her dad and looked him straight in the eye.

"Because, Dad, if I think too much - if Gute, Jazmin and I think, sweat and plan every little funky, clunky, stupid detail - we'll defeat ourselves before we start. Do you know why dad?"

Tom Hawk hated when his daughter acted recklessly, as she was, but he did love her intensity, he could never deny that.

"No, Mandalay, I don't know why."

"Because dad, we're just winging it. We're going to have an encounter with the powers that be - the mayor, the governor, whoever shows up. But beyond that - we have no money and we're doing it without any adult help. We've focused all our time on studying the science of global warming. We know it cold, pardon the pun." She smirked for a split second, then resumed: "And getting the word out about our, uhm … *encounter* – we got that covered. The word is out, trust me. Lots of kids say they're coming."

"Why won't you tell me exactly what you're planning?"

"Because you'll think we're crazy, that's why."

"But I'm your father."

"Sorry. This is a kids' thing. We have to be on our own. We have to do it solo and we have to be different."

Mandalay's dad took a deep, frustrated breath and shook his head in despair.

"And this is the reason why, dad. Because we're not doing what's already been done. Those climate strikes and huge protest rallies with all those millions of kids and talking heads years ago - *they all failed.* All the scientists, all the environmentalists, and all those amazing kids who did a great job about 10 years ago - *they all failed.* We have to do something different, *much different.*"

She paused for a few seconds, took a noticeable breath.

"It's 99 degrees in dumberbummersummer. We're swimming

year round in the Hudson River, southern climate refugees are flooding into New York and the city now has canals like Venice. The Bronx Zoo doesn't exist anymore and the southern part of Manhattan is under water. In 20 years, the entire city may be under water. And this is just New York. What about the rest of the country, or the rest of the world? We're living crazy - *every day*. What has been done to stop global warming? Treaties and laws come and go like clouds blowing in the wind. The government denies man-made climate change or just doesn't do enough to stop it. Rallies are held, but movements fizzle out. Companies just want to make money, because they don't care. If we continue down this path, half the world will either be starving to death or be forced to migrate. Wars from our past will look like dart throwing contests compared to what's coming in the future. All this – *why*? Because climate change is rampaging, galloping across our earth.

"So I'm going to sweat a lot. But I'm not going to sweat the details. And we're not repeating what came before us."

Mandalay had said what she had to say. And Tom Hawk had listened, and heard what he had to hear from his daughter. Despite his fear of her failing, of her getting in trouble, he believed in her, believed in his wild, yet very smart, articulate and precocious 14-year-old daughter. He really did. And she believed in herself.

"Sweetheart, you heard there's even crazier weather coming down in the next 24 hours - the day of your event, right?" her father had to ask. "It could be kind of serious."

"Yes, of course dad, I know. We'll deal with it," she said, lying, because she had not checked the weather report. She was just too busy studying and handing out fliers.

She felt ready for the *encounter* the next day.

Chapter 13: What?

THERE WAS NO SCIENTIST ON earth who could have predicted what would happen next.

At about 2 am, Mandalay was sound asleep when a loud crashing noise woke her up. She jerked up from her bed and realized there was a huge hole in her window and a howling wind outside. Then she realized she was covered in glass.

"Dad!" she screamed. He came rushing in and flicked on the light.

"Oh my God, Mandalay," he said, "don't move!" He saw glass strewn all over her floor and a baseball-size hail ball smack in the middle of her room. And then he saw all the blood and glass covering her arms and face. "Don't move!" he repeated, this time much more loudly.

Mandalay looked down and saw her glass-and blood-covered arms and turned as white as a ghost.

"Dad - I'm bleeding!" a panicked Mandalay shouted.

"Don't worry," he said, "I'm going to carry you out of here."

He tiptoed around the glass with his bare feet, picked her up off the bed, carried her into the living room and placed her on the couch. He looked out the window and heard the wind and saw the chaos - shattered windows all over, ambulances screaming around town, and realized he would have to tend to Mandalay's wounds himself. He once was an EMT - so he knew what to do.

He quickly gathered gauze, towels, disinfectant, a basin of warm water and as many Band-Aids as he could find.

"Dad - that hurts!" Mandalay screamed, as he began cleansing the wounds on her arms and face with a warm wet cloth and then some iodine.

"You're really lucky darling, these are all superficial cuts," he said, as she cried a little with each gentle wipe. "I know it stings, but you'll be fine. Fortunately the glass missed your eyes."

News reports called it the *Hail from Hell*. The hail balls whipped across the city with ferocious winds, denting cars, cracking windows and smashing skulls. More than 10,000 windows were smashed, more than 1,000 people were hospitalized and 59 people died after being hit on the head with hail. But then, unbelievably, it got worse. The record-breaking rainfall that fell after the hail stopped - called simply *The Deluge* - was described by one famous writer this way:

It was as if an infinite number of 100-foot giants with buckets the size of football stadiums stood above the city dumping water. With 80 mile-an-hour winds, an ocean cascaded down upon us.

The Deluge lasted two hours. Thirteen inches of rain fell in Central Park, shattering the old record from 2029 of 10 inches. The canals in the city flooded over so that Manhattan became one huge lake. Dozens and dozens of people drowned as they were swept into the Hudson and East rivers. The city's water supply was contaminated.

When Mandalay, Gute, Jazmin and millions of other New Yorkers turned on their water faucets a few hours later, water didn't come out. What they got was a slow oozing of dark brown sludge.

New York City's Water Will Make You Sick! Don't Drink The Water! all the warnings shouted on the internet, radio, TV and even from loudspeakers attached to police boats cruising the city.

The water was contaminated because flood waters carried sewage into the city's reservoirs.

So there was no water to drink for millions of people. Showers were not allowed. This went on for days.

The temperature rose to 108 degrees. The hospitals were flooded with thousands of people - those injured by large hail balls and thousands more who got sick from dehydration. Because no one was allowed to shower, everyone smelled terribly, like dead fish rotting in the streets.

The city tried to distribute three bottles of drinking water per day per person. Mandalay's father asked for and got one extra bottle a day to clean Mandalay's wounds. She had little scabs all over her face and arms, but she was recovering well.

Don't go outside, Don't move around!!! was the headline in *The Sunny Day News.*

> *"A state of emergency is declared in New York City because of the floods, the water shortage and the intense heat,"* Mayor Louise Goldberg El-Hassan announced. *"New Yorkers are not allowed to leave their homes unless they need to go to the hospital or need to buy food. You must conserve energy and stay out of the heat. If you are caught out of your home and don't have a proper excuse, you'll be arrested."*

Mandalay sat in her room, slowly sipped her bottled water, sweated through one t-shirt after another and stewed. She felt short of breath. A sharp pain shot from her shoulders to her neck, into her head - and it had nothing to do with the 19 cuts on her body from the flying glass or the sweat dripping down her face and stinging those cuts. She closed her eyes. She could not believe what she had read ... or what was happening. *Is this some crazy nightmare?* she thought. Because the article had gone on to explain that all this was caused by the very thing Mandalay, Gute and Jazmin were trying to stop.

> *"Well, of course, climate change is the reason for this unexpected and seemingly inexplicable hail, deluge and extreme heat,"* explained Macko Bilko, distinguished professor of meteorology at Penn State University. *"We call this a once-in-a-thousand-year storm - except it happened in Germany last week, too. Global warming causes ultra-extreme weather at unexpected times – and that's what we have now. It reminds us what hell looks like and what our future will be unless we do something immediately to stop it."*

How pathetic was this, Mandalay thought, *because it was global warming that had shut them down, cancelled their encounter, forced them to stay home.*

At about midnight two days later, Mandalay had had enough. She zapped Jazmin.

I'm coming over we need to figure this out

But when she got to the front door, she saw something unexpected.

The front door to her apartment was padlocked shut. Unbeknownst to her, her father had installed the lock - and he had the only key. The note taped to the door said:

Mandalay: I love you, but sometimes I need to take steps to protect you. If you get arrested outside the apartment, Judge Baxter could send you up the river. Stay home, go to sleep. You'll have plenty of time to save the world. I do love you. Dad

Her dad was sound asleep. So Mandalay lay on her bed and wrote this letter to him:

Dad: I love you too. I'm in my bedroom, staying home like you asked (did I have a choice?). But I'm just letting you know, as I already explained, that there is not one thing in the world that will stop me from what I have set out to do. Our NYC encounter may have been smashed by ice balls from hell, but our world encounter is a coming. Please DO NOT try to stop me. Like I said, I do love you. your daughter, Mandalay!

For the next few days, she was thirsty, smelly, angry and getting ready to blast off like a rocketship. She didn't even care that she went the last day of water rationing without a drop of water for the last six hours. Her mouth felt like she had swallowed a bottle of sand.

PART 4: WILL THEY SINK OR SWIM?

Chapter 1: Politicians and adults really ...

AFTER A WEEK, THE CITY began to recover. The flood waters receded, the mess was cleaned up and the water supply was purified and fixed. New Yorkers could drink normal amounts of water again.

But since the tsunami sauna stayed with them - it was 104 degrees in the shade - water rationing for bathing was imposed: A person could shower twice a week, for 90 seconds.

Mandalay still had small scabs all over her face and arms. As she dripped sweat and walked through the hall to class, Mr. Harkness appeared out of nowhere, shoved a large envelope into Mandalay's hands, looked at her wounds, mumbled something like "Poor girl," and kept on walking.

"Mr. Harkness handed me this like it was a spy movie or something," Mandalay told Gute and Jazmin later, holding up the envelope.

"We're glad you're ok," Jazmin said, as Gute patted Mandalay on the back.

"Thanks," a focused Mandalay said, as she ripped open the envelope and pulled out a stack of white papers. A handwritten note on top said: *This is your secret weapon.*

Mandalay rolled her eyes as she leafed through the thick documents. She saw they were articles written by a Professor Efram Zumwalt.

"Jeez, I guess we're supposed to read this stuff," Mandalay sighed, looking at her friends.

"I thought we were all done studying," Gute said.

"I have a hunch, we're never done," Jazmin said.

At lunch, Mandalay, Gute and Jazmin put on their floppy sunhats, sprayed themselves with Sunkiller and took a walk in Central Park.

"I know what we need to do," Mandalay said, about five seconds after they entered the park. "I've had plenty of time to think about it."

She stopped walking, turned to face her friends and explained her plan.

"But if we use the word suck, it will piss off a lot of people," Jazmin said.

"That's the point," Mandalay shot back. "We have to piss off as many people as possible."

They printed up hundreds of fliers at Gute's:

Time to March on Washington
KRAAP – Kids Revolt Against Adult Power!!!

*Adults suck. Politicians suck. Truly, honestly, they all really, really, **really** suck, because after more than 40 years, they have failed to stop global warming, and it's about to get much worse. Will the next hail storm smash our buildings, will forest fires burn them down, or will the hurricanes just blow them away? Will floods sink our cities and contaminate our drinking water forever, or will droughts just suck us dry and make living impossible? It's all caused by all those carbon emissions, causing this HOLY MESS of scorching temps, deadly weather, melting ice caps, rising seas, all leading to mass migration, starvation, disease, food wars, wildfires, etc. Adults caused it, time for kids to fix it.*

***KRAAP – Kids Revolt Against Adult Power!!!** Kids ages 13-16, march on Washington, D.C., May 15, 2031. 9 am, 110th and Broadway. Bring sleeping bag, extra socks, poncho, first aid stuff, toilet paper, sunkiller, sunhats, a towel and three days food and water.*

THIS IS AN EMERGENCY!!!
THIS IS AN ENCOUNTER!!!
We're not leaving Washington without a deal!!!

Mandalay Hawk, Jazmin Morjani and Gute Patooma

They had a month to spread the word. Every day after school they stuffed their backpacks with fliers, grabbed their stink towels and crisscrossed NYC's five boroughs by foot, boat, kayak, and subway. They drank gallons of water and got huge blood blisters on their feet from walking dozens and dozens of blocks a day. They smelled really badly, but they didn't care. They stood outside the city's high schools and handed out fliers to every student they saw ages 13-16. (They decided on this age group, their age group, because they wanted kids who were somewhat independent, but not old enough to be seen as threatening to adults.) They went to community centers and ball fields, bodegas and apartment buildings, migrant centers and to the Hudson River swimming hole.

Their cancelled NYC encounter was a thing in the distant past. The enthusiasm seemed high. Kids read the flier, then zapped the word around. Word was spreading, big-time.

"What if more than 100,000 kids join us? What if it's like a million kids?" Gute wondered, with a silly grin on his face.

"That means we'll need about a million pizzas a night to feed us," Jazmin said, with mock seriousness.

"And a million quarts of ice cream – *a day*," Mandalay added, rolling her eyes.

They didn't realize that the day of the march was the same day as the first National Tech IQ Test, a test mandatory in every middle school and high school in America.

Chapter 2: Uh oh ...

PRINCIPAL BUSHWICK WAS CLUELESS ABOUT their plan until late one night, when his ring pinged. A parent had gotten hold of a flier, photographed it and zapped it to him.

"Principal Bushwick, are you going to let these three juvenile delinquents get away with this? ARE YOU??!!" It was signed: **An anonymously concerned UNsucky parent.**

He read the flier. Then he read it again.

*Did these three kids, these three delinquents in **his** school, just say that all adults suck, that these sucky, sucky adults were to blame for global warming, and that students in **his** school should cut school to march on Washington? ON THE DAY OF THAT MANDATORY NATIONAL TECH IQ TEST!!*

Bushwick hated when kids messed with his school ... especially when it messed up an important plan. He also happened to be one of those sucky adults who had stopped caring about global warming. He believed the recent crazy weather was not the new norm - but more like a once in a lifetime event. When he called his brother in Maine in the middle of the night, he said, "Hubert, the temperature has dropped to 97 degrees. It's really not so hot out anymore."

Hubert said: "You see, she's messing with you too! She's a punk, a troublemaker. You must stop her!"

Homer said: "Don't worry, brother, I'll take care of her – and her friends."

Chapter 3: A double whammy!

B USHWICK'S ZAP TO THEIR PARENTS began with the words:

**WARNING: YOUR CHILD IS ABOUT TO BE
EXPELLED FROM HEMINGWAY HIGH**
*They are forbidden from leading this march and forbidden
from encouraging kids to skip school and
miss the* **MANDATORY TEST!!!**

He attached a copy of their flier.

Jazmin's mom saw the zap first. She called Mandalay's dad and Gute's dad.

"This is not happening. These kids are not marching to Washington. I don't give a crap what's at stake," Jazmin's mom snorted angrily.

The parents demanded a meeting that night with their kids. They met at Mandalay's apartment. It didn't begin with hugs and kisses.

"Are you kidding me!" Jazmin's mom screeched at her daughter, and at Gute and Mandalay, holding a copy of the flier. *"Adults suck! That's really, really nice. And march to Washington? In this heat, without adult supervision? A bunch of teenage babies - are you kidding me!?! You want to die!!??!!"*

Tom Hawk placed a comforting hand on her shoulder.

"Yes, we're concerned," he said softly, trying to calm the situation. "We think your goal is a little unrealistic."

Mandalay cleared her throat. "We knew this would piss you off, which is why we didn't tell you. But you have to understand: We *are* marching to Washington, because we have to. Bushwick thinks we're taking over his school … that stupid test. You think we're endangering ourselves. But the truth is, if we don't march to Washington and demand change, we're endangering the world.

"No offense dad, and no offense to any adults," Mandalay continued, as she shook her head at the three parents standing in front of her, "but the adults of the world blew it, we're living through hell, it will only get worse, so yeah, adults suck for blowing it – *sorry* – and we're going to fix this problem, once and for all."

There were a few moments of silence. Then a few more. Tom Hawk had warned Gute's dad and Jazmin's mom about his daughter, that she was unusually stubborn, unusually motivated and would not take no for an answer. But still …

"This is a noble effort, really, it is," Gute's dad said, also trying to remain calm, while talking some sense into these kids. "But you'll be expelled from school. And have you thought about what will be needed to march with hundreds or thousands of young teenagers 200 miles in 100-plus degree heat? Have you actually thought that through?"

"And my God!" Jazmin's mom angrily shot out. "Have you actually thought about what you'll do if by some miracle on earth you get to Washington? Do you think the president is just sitting on his butt, waiting to have a picnic with a bunch of teenagers?"

Of course, these were the gazillion dollar questions that had flitted briefly through their minds while studying and passing out fliers: *food? water? where to sleep? details, shmetails …*

"The truth is, we talked about these issues a little," Mandalay said.

"A little!?!" Jazmin's mother shrieked, again.

"Well, yeah, just a little," Jazmin explained, "because we focused on studying, not the logistics."

"Because we think the details will work out," Gute added. "Somehow …"

"Really, son, just like magic?" Gute's dad asked, finally losing his patience. "Are you a bunch of two-year olds?"

Mandalay had heard enough. "No, we're not a bunch of two-year olds," she shot back. "We're teenagers with a conscience, which is more than I can say for your generation." She pulled out a piece of paper from her pocket and unfolded it. "How's this gonna fly when this happens?" She shoved it towards the parents. It was a printout of an article with the headline:

Water rationing and food shortages predicted for most of U.S. by 2035

"Still think we're crazy?"

Tom Hawk was listening, hand to chin, trying to remain calm. He took a deep breath.

There were a few moments of angry silence. "I think the parents need to talk," he finally suggested.

So they did. For a good, solid hour. And when they were done, Jazmin's mom shook her head and said: "It's too dangerous, Jazmin, I forbid you from going."

Gute's dad: "Son, you're not going, either."

Both parents stood there defiantly, with arms crossed.

Then there was death-rattling silence for a few moments. If someone listened closely, they could hear the three kids breathing *… and thinking.*

Mandalay looked at her friends. They looked at her. Then Jazmin looked at Gute, and Gute looked at Jazmin. They didn't say a word to each other, because they didn't need to.

"Sorry mom, I love you, but I'm marching to Washington," Jazmin said, shaking her head up and down. "And you can't stop me."

"Dad, I'm going, too," said Gute, also nodding. "We made a commitment to each other. This is too important."

The parents didn't know what to say. They looked at Mandalay and gave her a hard, nasty stare. Tom Hawk never said a word. Because he knew better. There was no way they were going to stop his daughter. So why bother trying.

Chapter 4: Granny pushes Billy over the edge

GERTRUDE JOHNSON COULDN'T HELP GET them to Washington. But she sure as heck could help them once they got there.

She had heard about the flyer, because word was spreading.

She was no dummy. She knew action was needed now.

And she knew that dear grandson Billy sometimes took his sweet old time doing things he didn't want to do. Billy had been delaying, hoping against hope the favor asked by granny would just go away, fly off into outer space somehow. But the hail and deluge came, and now the favor requested was more like an urgent demand.

Billy was at home one night, just outside Washington, D.C., when he got the call from granny. He listened on the phone and took a deep, nervous breath.

"Ok granny, I understand."

He listened, his stomach churning nervously.

"Yes, of course I love you."

He listened some more.

"Ok. Ok, Ok. Yes, I understand."

A few days later, it was mid-afternoon, and Billy was at work, in our nation's capital.

Sara and Bergen were at home doing homework in the net room. Billy stood outside the room nervously biting his finger-nails. Now was as good a time as any. He had a captured audience. He knocked.

"Hi, Billy, wassup?" asked Sara.

"I need to talk with you," Billy said.

Billy rarely asked to talk with them privately. In fact, he had done it only twice before: once, when a man scaled the White House fence and was not caught for a few minutes. And a second time, when the president was rushed to the hospital because he had fainted.

Billy was in the Secret Service. Sara, 15, and Bergen, 13, were the daughters of President William "Bucky" Billingham. Billy had been in charge of their protection for 2 ½ years, since the president was elected in November 2028.

"Listen girls," Billy said. "I have something important to talk to you about."

He paused, because what he was about to say next he had never said before.

"I would ask you, please, don't tell anyone what I'm going to say."

Those words hung in the air. Billy was not allowed to say that to these girls, and Sara and Bergen knew it.

"That's against the rules," Sara said.

"Are you a spy, Billy? Because if you are, we'll have to tell our dad," added Bergen.

It was against the law - *yes, against the law* – for there to be secrets.

"No, I'm not a spy. My granny ..."

Sara and Bergen immediately looked at each and rolled their eyes.

They had heard about granny, particularly the time when she was brought to the Oval Office for a photo, but instead lectured the president about civil rights.

"Ok, I know what you're thinking, but my granny is amazing, and when she asks me to do something ..."

"You can't say no," Sara and Bergen said at the same time, laughing.

"Well, yeah. It's a big favor." He paused. "Have you heard of Mandalay Hawk?"

Chapter 5: The Torture Chamber

HUNDREDS AND HUNDREDS OF FLIERS were passed around, kid to kid, then parent to parent. The message went wide as kids zapped and rezapped like crazy. But there were two big problems with the whole thing. First, most politicians and adults still didn't care enough about climate change, even though it was broiling and causing havoc. And using the word *suck* had backfired big time.

"How dare those kids say all adults suck. How dare they! No way are you leaving this house to march with those delinquents. No way!!!" Those parental words echoed across New York City.

And, of course, Bushwick had decided that their *sucky* plan did, in fact, *suck*.

No matter the baking planet. No matter that it would be 103 in the shade that afternoon. No matter nothin'. The combo of Bushwick's rage and parental opposition turned Hemingway High into a sweltering, smelly torture chamber.

"We support you 100 percent. We'll be there in spirit, but our parents won't allow us to march."

They must have heard that line 50 times.

"We support you in spirit."

"A lot of good that will do us," Mandalay said to Gute and Jazmin.

"We told our parents off, why can't they?" Jazmin said angrily.

"Because they don't have the guts we have," Gute said.

And plastered all over school, in fact, plastered all over virtually every middle and high school in New York City were signs with the following words:

Warning: *If you skip school to march on Washington, D.C., on May 15th and miss the MANDATORY TECH IQ TEST, you will be suspended from school and have to repeat your current grade. If you lead the march and encourage kids to miss school, you will be EXPELLED. Attendance on May 15th is* **MANDATORY**.

To say that Mandalay, Gute and Jazmin had lowered their expectations would be an understatement.

"If 100 kids march with us that would be good," Mandalay said to her friends, but then realized that would not be enough to raise a proper ruckus. *Not even close.* But they were not going to give up.

After many late nights, they had finally finished reading the Zumwalt papers given to them by Mr. Harkness. They were a detailed scientific analysis about renewable energy: power generated by the sun (solar power), by wind (wind power) and by water (water power, aka hydroelectric power). Then Mandalay, Gute and Jazmin stayed up late discussing it. They had read a lot about renewable energy before. But Zumwalt's detailed plan was still an eye opener. It added to everything they had learned the past few months studying their butts off.

They would ram all this information down the president's throat – if they got the chance.

If they got to Washington.

If they made it out of New York with enough kids to make enough noise to be heard above the clamoring tourists.

If, if, if …
A lot of freakin' ifs.

Chapter 6: Mr. Harkness
to the rescue, again

I T WAS NOW TWO DAYS before the march. They were exhausted, like walking zombies at school. Students eyeballed them, nodded, half smiled, but kept their distance ... and just stopped talking to them.

The heat had not let up. It was another 105 degree May day. Because of the recent water contamination, the school's water fountains were still clogged with brown sludge and didn't work. This meant bottled water only and a principal who had tunnel vision and didn't care.

"We must stop these delinquents at all costs. Kids are not allowed to miss that test!" he demanded of the teachers at an emergency meeting, as sweat dripped down his face. "No exceptions!" Mr. Harkness heard those words, closed his eyes and shook his head.

He immediately held a secret meeting with other teachers at school.

Later, when history class began, Mr. Harkness closed the door, locked it and pulled down the shades so no one could enter or look in. Then he said to his class: "In 48 hours, three of your classmates will embark on an historic mission. I know most of you feel obliged to obey your parents. Everyone is afraid of making a mistake – of screwing up and getting tossed out of school. But this march, *this encounter, this thing they are doing,* is far more important than any of your own worries."

He paused, took a breath and then continued.

"It couldn't be much hotter, could it?" he asked his class, removing his folded stink towel from his desk drawer and wiping his sweaty face. "Now is the time to take a stand - *to revolt* - and make some serious noise! Before it's really too late."

His class had become drop dead quiet, except for the creaky fans blowing hot air around the room. Mr. Harkness was usually this elderly, mild-mannered history teacher (except when a student slept in his class), and mostly a by-the-book guy. Except when he got ticked off.

"And by the way, I don't give a hoot what Bushwick thinks," Mr. Harkness added, staring intently at his students.

"So, who's marching with Mandalay, Gute and Jazmin?!" he asked forcefully and impatiently, looking around expectantly at the 30 kids in front of him.

There was silence. No one raised their hand. The silence stretched to 10, 15 … 30 seconds.

Mr. Harkness shook his head in frustration. "Ok."

He approached the first row of students.

"Alexander?"

Alexander was shy to begin with, but this was too much pressure. He was trying to stare a hole in the floor.

"My mom says if I mess up I won't get into college," he said, in barely a whisper.

"Beth?"

"I … I … I … I have … have perfect attendance," Beth stammered nervously. "And I want t t t t to g g go go go t t t to a a a goo goo goo good c c c college."

Mr. Harkness shook his head again.

"Thomas?"

He shrugged his shoulders, shook his head, and looked at the floor.

"My dad said …"

He did not finish his sentence.

On and on it went.

"My mom said …"

"My dad said …"

The tech IQ test, Bushwick's threat, fear of getting in trouble – all hanging over their heads like a humongous boulder dangling by a thread.

Classmate after classmate.

"You must be kidding me!" Harkness finally blurted out angrily, shaking his head. Then he picked up his water bottle, opened the top and drank the last few drops. "So now if I want to go fill it up again, I can't."

The class looked on in silence. "But this is nothing compared to what's gonna happen to us or what's going on in other parts of the world. It's so hot and dry in Africa they can't grow enough food to feed half the people. The U.S. might have the same problem in a few years." He stood there with his hands in the air, holding his empty water bottle upside down. A last, single drop dripped out and Harkness caught it in his mouth.

He stared at the class for a moment, then said angrily, "You're not treating this like the earth emergency it is." He approached the back row. "I think you're all way too scared of your parents or of Bushwick. Who cares what they think if the heat we feel every single day is actually killing us?"

Mandalay, Gute and Jazmin felt badly that Mr. Harkness was coming down so hard on their classmates. If they didn't want to march …

But then a girl, in the back row, said quietly, "I think I'm going." It was Sally Dutton.

"*You think?*" Mr. Harkness said, in no mood for uncertainty.

"Well, my parents forbid me from going," Sally said, a little louder, "then I thought about it, and realized, I had no choice. After all" – she giggled from embarrassment – "it's the best thing for my children and my grandchildren."

That broke the ice. Everyone in class laughed, because the thought of Sally with children and grandchildren seemed pretty gross to everyone.

"When I told my parents I was going to march, my dad said that he loved me very much and that because he did, he was grounding me because he thought it was too dangerous for a 14-year-old kid to walk 200 miles in broiling heat without food and water. Plus, he said, if I got suspended, I wouldn't get into college and I'd never get a job."

Sally paused to catch her breath.

"But I said to not take this risk would make things worse, because it's only going to get hotter and the hotter the planet, the more that people will suffer. So I told my parents they could ground me, but that on May 15th I was walking out the door and marching to Washington."

Sally looked at Mandalay, then at Gute, then at Jazmin, and nodded.

And they were looking at Sally, thinking: *Wow, she's about the coolest kid in school.*

Then Mandalay stood up because she couldn't help herself. "Thanks Sally and thanks Mr. Hartwick." She felt a little weird about pushing kids, but she now felt she had no choice.

"Sally's right, you know," Mandalay said. "It makes no sense to listen to our parents and Bushwick to avoid getting kicked out of school, because really, what we are trying to avoid is getting kicked off earth. Because that's what's happening now."

Mandalay nodded confidently, because she knew she had said the right thing at the right time.

Jazmin stood up.

"Yeah, in fact, that expulsion from earth has already begun," she went on. "The average temperature in parts of France last week was 114 degrees. *114 degrees.* In India, it was 128. *128. Twenty-five thousand people died in two days.*" She paused as she wiped sweat from her brow with her stink towel. "We have no choice. We have to march."

A half dozen kids then pledged they would march. More said they would think about it.

A similar thing happened in other classrooms, as many of the teachers also thought Bushwick was out of his mind. And then the teachers began zapping colleagues in other schools, so this scene was played out in classrooms and schools all across New York City.

But it was unclear how many kids would be joining Mandalay, Gute and Jazmin. Most kids said they were just too afraid.

Someone had zapped a KRAAP flier to that reporter Jonny Jackson, then a copy of the suspension/expulsion warning from school. "Jeeze," she mumbled as she marched through the newsroom towards her desk. She tried to avoid her editor, because the day before he assigned her to cover the mayor's annual turtle race in a Central Park cactus garden.

Chapter 7: A freeze dried dad

Tom Hawk had come to accept that his daughter – his very smart and very motivated, but extremely unprepared daughter - was going to try to march to Washington without any plan or parental support in this blistering heat. He knew he could not stop her. But he had hoped his daughter would at least ask for advice. But no, that didn't happen.

"Dad, remember, we have a deal. You said you trusted me," she said to him, as the march approached.

He had never seen her so determined. He tried to hide it, but he was getting more and more worried.

Two nights back he woke up at 3 am in a panic, drenched in sweat from a scary dream: he got a zap from a ghost saying something had gone horribly wrong, that Mandalay and her friends were lost and starving on some lonely country road in the middle of nowhere.

So, the day before Mandalay was to start her march, Tom Hawk left work early, not to go home to cook one last dinner for Mandalay, but to go downtown to a camping store.

"Where are the micromini-GPS trackers?" he asked the clerk, as soon as he entered.

He found the one he read about on the net, the smallest one with a global reach, for $1,399.

"*Used by the CIA and FBI to track terrorists and spies,*" the package said.

It could be hidden in Mandalay's backpack and she wouldn't even know it. Tom Hawk would always know where his daughter was. *Always.*

He then loaded up his cart with enough freeze dried food to

feed a small army: pasta primavera, beef stroganoff, vegetable stir fry, and chili, then added freeze dried berries and ice cream. Then he grabbed socks, lots of extra cushioned socks for long hikes.

He didn't care that the bill came to $1,871. But as he was carrying the bulky bags out of the store, he realized that perhaps he, not Mandalay, was the one who truly was nuts.

So what that her plan for eating consisted of bananas, granola bars, a half dozen bottles of water and a prayer. She was trying to stop the biggest problem earth had ever faced.

And what if Mandalay found that tracking device?

And even if she didn't find it, what did this say about his trust for his daughter?

He stood on the street outside the store and thought for a few minutes. He looked around, not at anyone, but at and into his own soul. He took a deep, deep breath. Thought some more ... then turned around and returned all the stuff he had just bought, except the socks.

"Hi sweetheart," Tom Hawk said later, when Mandalay walked into the apartment, smiling, looking surprisingly relaxed for a girl about to start a trek akin to hiking across the Sahara Desert.

"That smells great, dad, what did you make me?" Mandalay asked, as she hugged her dad.

"Your favorite, sweetheart. I figured you needed a good last meal to get you going." He had rushed to the grocery store after his visit to the camping store.

"So how's it going?" Tom Hawk asked, not wanting to be too nosy, as he stirred the tomato sauce and began plopping ravioli into the boiling water.

"Well," Mandalay said, thinking about how to answer, "Bushwick is trying to kill us and most of the parents in New York City think we're idiots. It's possible a few hundred kids will join us." Then she added, "But, I really have no idea. Some kids say they're coming. Their parents may chain them to their beds. I have no clue."

Tom Hawk nodded. "I bought you a few things."

He handed Mandalay a small bag with the socks and a small box with a purple ribbon.

"Dad …"

She smiled at the socks. "Thanks, I needed these." Then she removed the box from the bag, untied the ribbon and opened the box. She stared at what was inside. "Dad, this is beautiful," Mandalay said. She ran her fingers over the shiny silver bracelet, the silver squares connected by smaller silver links.

"Sweetheart, read the back," he said.

Mandalay turned it over and across the squares, in small print, the inscription read:

Mandalay: Our life's journey is always together, no matter how far apart we are. Love U, Dad

"It's so beautiful. I'll never take it off," she said, as she put on the bracelet. She hugged her dad tight, and he hugged her back.

Then the buzzer on the stove went off. The ravioli was ready.

They sat down for dinner and Mandalay ate like … well, like a teenager getting ready for a long, long, *long* march.

"The weather report looks good," her dad said, not wanting to wade into forbidden-discussion territory, like the total lack of planning.

"I've got plenty of water, because I know it will be hot," Mandalay said, nodding.

"I'm going to give you $200 cash so you have plenty of money in your pocket."

Mandalay looked up from her plate of ravioli.

"Wow, dad, that's very generous."

"You need to have cash. Just in case …"

Mandalay could see the concerned look on her father's face.

"Dad, this is all gonna be fine, don't worry, ok?" Mandalay said. "Somehow, this will all work out."

"What's that old kid's book, where the food falls out of the sky?" Tom Hawk asked, smiling.

"Oh yeah - *Cloudy with a Chance of Meatballs*." Mandalay laughed.

"Come to think of it, I did notice the weather report said something about global warming causing a rare weather phenomenon, with pancakes plopping to earth from outer space," he said.

"Yeah, with syrupy rain to follow, right dad?" Mandalay added. She balled up her napkin and playfully threw it at her dad.

"And a magic carpet will carry us to DC," she added with a mocking smile, nodding.

"Oh, I almost forgot to give you this," Tom Hawk said, taking an envelope out of his pocket and handing it to Mandalay. "This came in the mail."

Mandalay ripped open the envelope and found a note inside.

PLEASE PLEASE PLEASE zap Billy Johnson at @ bjohnson6666 - He will help you!! I PROMISE!!! Good luck, Gertrude Johnson

Mandalay waved the note at her dad. "Gertrude is a really sweet lady," Mandalay said. "She doesn't give up. But we don't need any adults mucking it up."

Chapter 8: A dozen hissing rattlesnakes

THE FIRST THING MANDALAY DID when she woke up the next morning was look out the window.

"No hail," she said out loud to herself jokingly and punched her fist in the air. The weather report had called for sunny and high of 103.

Mandalay moved through her morning routine and took her 90 second shower.

And adults still don't think there's a problem, Mandalay thought to herself, as she rushed to wash and rinse before the shower clicked off automatically.

For breakfast, Mandalay ate like a bear. She splattered double the normal amount of granola, chopped fruit, nuts and yogurt into a huge bowl and began stuffing her face.

"Good morning sweetheart," her dad said, as he entered the living room. He noticed Mandalay's intensity right away. She was chewing like a maniac, not smiling, just chewing quickly and staring out the window at a cloudless sky.

Mandalay nodded. She was trying to ignore those butterflies, the ones filling her body and being chased by a dozen hissing rattlesnakes.

Tom Hawk acted and looked calm, but inside he had his own bellyful, as if a thousand grasshoppers were inside trying to get out.

He had not slept well. He was still worried sick. But he didn't want Mandalay to know.

You just have to let go, he told himself - *whatever happens, happens.* Because he knew he could not stop her.

"Here darling," he said. First it was the socks and bracelet, now a brown paper bag filled with a cheese, tomato and seaweed wrap, and an apple, yogurt and granola bars.

He was loading up his daughter with *him* – if he couldn't go – things he gave her could.

"At least you'll have a decent lunch today," he said, clenching his jaw, trying to smile through nerves and emotions.

"Thanks dad, I love you," Mandalay said. She could see her dad was struggling, as he glanced at the silver bracelet on her wrist. She hugged him and held him tight for a minute. She was clutching the paper bag, as if it contained gold.

"I'm sure the lunch will be delicious," she said, as she cleared her throat of her own emotions.

Mandalay shoved the lunch, a bag of rice bagels, bananas and granola bars, her notebook, clothes, a sleeping bag and many bottles of water into her backpack and zipped it shut.

She looked at her dad, nodded, half smiled and lifted her heavy backpack onto her back. She quickly gave him one last hug.

"I'll see you in a few days … or in a week or two," she said. "You can follow us on the net, I hope."

"Ok," Tom Hawk managed, trying to smile, but saying little so as not to get too emotional.

Mandalay sprayed herself with Sunkiller. Then, instead of wearing her sunhat, she put on a special black baseball cap she had made for herself, Gute and Jazmin: In red letters, it said: *KRAAP Will Stop Global Warming!* She looked at her dad, waiting for his reaction. He looked, half-smiled and nodded. A lump in his throat stopped him from talking.

Mandalay nodded with her own lump. "Bye dad, I love you," she said, then she walked out the door and down the steps into a sunny, hot - *very hot* - May day.

Chapter 9: The march is on!

MANDALAY HAD ONLY A FEW blocks to walk south to the deli on Broadway at 110th Street, where she was meeting Gute and Jazmin. She walked fast. Her mind was a tangled jumble of nerves and thoughts:

Howmanykidsaregonnamarchtodcwithus?Willtheyha veenoughfoodandwater?Aretheygonnasleepinanewjerseys wamp?Willanyonefaintbecauseoftheheat?Jeezelouisewill anyonelistentous?Anyone?

HOONNNNNNNNKK!!! was the first thing Mandalay heard. Then screeching tires.

Oh God!!! ... Mandalay jumped to the side.

The car had skidded to a stop about a foot from Mandalay. She had almost been hit, had walked right through a red light, never saw the car coming. Mandalay's heart was pounding through her chest.

"Are you blind?!!" the driver shouted.

Mandalay was shaken, but she had to move on. She took a deep breath and kept walking south.

When she arrived at the deli Nomad's, her first thought was that she was at the wrong place, because no one was there. Then she looked around and saw Gute and Jazmin, wearing their black KRAAP hats, sharing a wrap and Gatorade on a nearby bench, and then she saw four other kids standing on top of a flipped garbage can taking zelfies.

Great, Mandalay thought, *30 minutes before the march, and there are seven marchers, including four jokers who probably won't make it to Jersey.*

"How on earth are we gonna control this massive crowd?" Mandalay joked to her friends, motioning to the empty sidewalk around her.

"I mean, if we had planned to have food for 10,000 kids," she said, "we would have been off by only 9,993."

They looked around and shrugged it off.

"At least we know the facts of climate change," Gute said.

"Yeah, and this will be a lot easier, because we won't have to worry about anyone else, unless you count those four," Jazmin said, shaking her head at the kids clowning around.

"So how many miles are we gonna walk each day?" said a new kid, now the eighth marcher, who was so small he looked nine, except he had some peach fuzz on his upper lip.

This question brought them a little smack of reality. *Yeah, they were in charge.* However many kids showed up, they would look to them for leadership.

Mandalay wasn't sure what to say, because they had avoided talk of planning like you avoid hairy, scampering rats on the subway.

"We don't need to know how many miles a day we'll walk, because we're just going to walk until we get there," Mandalay told the little kid, speaking in a strong, confident voice, as she tried to hide her belly filled with more butterflies and snakes than an African jungle.

Then Mandalay, Gute and Jazmin got a little jolt. It wasn't a million, or even 10,000, but it was something.

After a long subway delay, a number 1 train pulled into the 110th Street station. And a boat bus pulled into the nearby dock. Within a few minutes 10, then 20, then 50 kids were on the street – kids of all colors, shapes, and sizes, all young teenagers carrying backpacks and sleeping bags.

Within ten minutes, they had 100 marchers.

Just like that, there was a buzz in the air.

"So where's Mandalay, Jazmin and Guck?" one kid shouted out.

Gute rolled his eyes at his friends.

"Hey, the name is *Gute*, and we're over here!" Gute yelled back, as they entered the crowd. All eyes were now on them, and for the first time they could sense the excitement.

"So when are we leaving?" another kid shouted.

This was up to them.

"I heard that subways and boats are delayed," a third kid said.

"So that means we can expect another 100,000 kids," Mandalay responded. "At least!"

"Really?" asked one small, freckled-faced girl, who looked too young to march.

Mandalay put her hand on her shoulder. "No, I was kidding."

The girl looked so young and innocent Mandalay wondered if she should be going.

"What's your name?" Mandalay asked.

"Daisy," she said. "I hope we leave soon, because I don't want my parents coming up here and taking me home."

"How old are you Daisy?" Mandalay asked.

Daisy shrugged her shoulders.

"I'm not going to tell anybody," Mandalay whispered, as she moved closer to her.

Daisy hesitated, then whispered back, "I'm eleven, but ... but I know all about how global warming is melting the ice caps and causing the seas to rise and, thereby, causing flooding in low-lying areas, and causing drought, famine and massive human migration and the epidemic spread of disease and, all in all, presenting a bleak future for our children and our children's children ... and ... and adults don't seem to give a hoot."

Daisy took a breath.

"Wow," Mandalay said, in awe. "Are you sure you're just eleven? You really know your stuff."

Mandalay turned to her friends. "Let's get going, before parents come here and grab their kids and drag them home." She knew with young teens, this could happen.

Mandalay, Gute and Jazmin began walking through the crowd, towards the front. The crowd kept growing.

The next boat pulled in and unloaded another 100 marching kids ... actually, it was about 200 kids by the time they all made it off the dock. Then another subway, followed by another boat. Boats and subways can arrive in rapid succession at rush hour and it was that time, as 9 am approached. The kids, milling about, filled the sidewalk between 110th and 112th streets on Broadway and were overflowing onto the street.

Before they knew it, there were more than 500 kids clogging the sidewalk and street. Honking cars could not pass.

There was the junior explorer's club from Neil Armstrong High School, all dozen members wearing hiking boots and khaki sunhats and carrying enough food and water for three days.

There were three dudes from the East Village, in flip flops, purple hats and tank tops with enough food and water until dinner, maybe, and the JV basketball team from Canarsie High in Brooklyn ... and young teens from all over the city.

This included the large crew from Hemingway High – several dozen kids, including Sally and others from Mr. Harkness's class, who had the guts to tell their parents to take a hike.

The deli, Nomad's, sold out of rice bagels, rice muffins and water, so the crowd turned to neighboring stores: Morningside Market; a seaweed place, Weed of the Sea; and an Italian wrap shop, Venizia Delizioso.

What had been a quiet, calm scene 30 minutes ago was now bustling and loud, with teens clamoring away, taking zelfies with their rings and clogging the sidewalk and street.

A shop owner came out into the street and wondered what in God's name was going on.

Mandalay jumped on top of a bench.

Jazmin took out a train whistle she brought along and blew it several times.

"Quiet please!" Mandalay shouted, holding up her hands. "Quiet please!"

She looked out on an expanding crowd, a crowd they never imagined.

"This is amazing!" Mandalay yelled to the kids clogging the street, as she looked north, then south on Broadway. As more and more subways and boats arrived, the crowd had grown to approximately 750. "We're about to embark on a journey that will be heard around the world."

Mandalay looked at her friends after saying those words.

"*Really?*" Gute mouthed to Jazmin. "*Heard around the world?*"

Mandalay was more hoping than predicting, as she shrugged at her friends.

"We're going to march on Washington and we're going to stay there until the president agrees to our demands!" she exclaimed. "We have no choice, they have no choice – the human race has no choice. Global warming must be stopped - *now!*"

Wow, that was pretty darn good, Jazmin thought, as the crowd continued to swell - now close to 1,000.

"Stop Global Warming!" one kid yelled out.

And then it was five kids yelling: "*Stop Global Warming!*"

Then 10, then 20, then 50.

Within 15 seconds, hundreds of kids were shouting:

Stop Global Warming!!!
Stop Global Warming!!!

The chant grew louder and louder as the crowd began marching north on Broadway, past rows of towering palm trees.

Stop Global Warming!!!
Stop Global Warming!!!
Stop Global Warming!!!

They picked up speed as more and more kids arrived, some well prepared with several day's food, sleeping bags and tents, and some with barely enough food for the day and dressed as if it was an afternoon trip to the beach.

Mandalay noticed this, but tried not to worry. They marched past Columbia University. Mandalay could not help but think of the famous people who had walked that campus, including President Obama, who had tried to build world momentum to stop global warming, but then it had been a roller coaster ride of bad, good and then more bad decisions about fighting climate change … And then *The Big Heat* settled in.

The chant grew louder as they marched north.

Stop Global Warming!!!
Stop Global Warming!!!
Stop Global Warming!!!

Shop owners came out to see what was going on. Traffic was clogged. Drivers honked and thrust thumbs up out their car windows in support.

It was 9:30, 92 degrees and going up. After more subways and boats arrived, the number of marchers had now increased to more than 2,000. They had 224 ½ miles to go.

Chapter 10: Governor Blowfish blows

THEY APPROACHED THE WEST SIDE Highway, which would lead them to the George Washington Bridge and then south to Washington. Mandalay expected rush hour traffic to stop and let this mass of teenagers hog the highway.

Not so fast, Mandalay realized, as cars and trucks whizzed by, ignoring them on the entrance ramp.

Mandalay jumped up on a ledge to address the still-growing number of marchers: "Listen, these cars are going 60 miles an hour and they don't want to stop. We'll have to convince them to jam on their brakes. Form rows of 10 kids across and lock arms. We're going to slowly – *very slowly* - march onto the highway. We'll occupy the road and march to the bridge."

Because this was still rush hour, closing in on 10 am, there was still a SHOUTNews helicopter overhead, filing traffic reports for net TV and radio every 10 minutes.

Mandalay, Gute and Jazmin and seven others were in the front row. Everyone behind them organized rows and locked arms.

The SHOUTNews reporter looked down and saw this unusual sight: a huge mass of people at the highway entrance ramp leading to the George Washington Bridge, stretching south for blocks. This would be the first official sighting of these kids.

"Something strange is going on down below, but I'm not sure what it is," the reporter said into his microphone. He would soon know.

The first car, then a second, then a third, and so on, had to screech to a halt as dozens of kids, then hundreds, with arms locked, marched slowly onto the highway. They filled the lanes. Cars had no choice but to stop.

"I'm not sure what this is, but what I can tell from above it looks like hundreds, perhaps thousands of young people, all wearing backpacks, are marching onto the West Side Highway," the reporter shouted into his microphone.

Little Daisy was actually holding Mandalay's hand so tight she was pinching the circulation.

"I'm scared," Daisy said.

"Don't worry," Mandalay replied. "Nothing's going to happen. I got you." She held Daisy's hand tight.

The growing crowd of now more than 3,000 marching kids had caused a massive traffic jam. Cars, unable to move an inch, were backing up south on the highway.

Mandalay chose the roadway merging to the upper deck on the George Washington Bridge, so the world could see them crossing one of the most famous bridges in America, and they would have a clear view south of Manhattan. If they were going to march 200-plus miles in blistering heat, they might as well see the sights.

"Pass it down," Gute said to the row behind him. "Look left and enjoy the view."

They passed it down … and down and down the message went. And what a view they all had.

The rippling Hudson River, and the shimmering Manhattan skyline in the distance, dozens of humongous skyscrapers, man-made stalactites, jutting towards the blue sky, sparkling in the early-morning sunlight, like a bedazzled Lego design.

They marched towards Jersey as the SHOUTNews chopper whirled above, broadcasting the march live. A parent had zapped SHOUTNews a flier.

"My gosh, these kids are awfully rude, saying all adults suck, even if they have a good cause," the reporter said into the microphone. "The question is: Will they make it through one night, before these teeny boppers start broiling and whining to mommy for a ride home? After all, it's gonna hit 105 today in Jersey, and no one but an alligator and a possum should be out in this heat."

Mandalay and the rest of her gang had no idea the reporter was making fun of them. And they were not in tune with the politics of New Jersey's Governor Blowfish. Governor Blowfish, a 350-pound former professional wrestler, was one nasty coot who cared deeply about traffic flow on the GW Bridge, because it connected Jersey to New York City. This bridge was his baby, his state's lifeline, and when something went wrong, he got royally pissed and threatened anyone in his way.

So, when he heard that there were thousands of teenagers on *his* bridge about to clog *his* New Jersey highways, he did the only thing he could think of.

He called in the National Guard.

To stop them cold and send these kids back to where they belonged: *school.*

"I don't want them messing up my roads, understand?" Governor Blowfish told Major Grunsky, the officer in charge. "Stop them! I want the roadway cleared by noon."

The National Guard set up an old fashioned road block on the Jersey side of the bridge. Hundreds of soldiers in camouflage uniforms with big guns and large army trucks blocked the road.

"Do you see what I see?" Gute said warily to Mandalay and Jazmin.

They held up their hands signaling for the marchers to stop. They were about 100 yards from the road block.

"This is not something I expected," Mandalay said, hands on hips. She paused for a few moments to figure out what to do. But only for a few moments.

She climbed up on the guardrail and shouted: "We're just going to walk right through."

"What do you mean, walk right through?" a kid in the fifth row shouted.

"I mean, they ain't gonna hit us, they sure as heck ain't gonna shoot us, and guess what, they ain't gonna stop us."

She pointed to the helicopter overhead, with its camera sticking out, broadcasting live to the world every second of what was about to happen.

"What do you think would happen if they put a hand on us - a bunch of kids - and the world saw what happened? Talk about a video flipping viral. All we do is say, 'Excuse me,' step around the soldiers and trucks, and keep right on walking. They can't – *they won't* - touch us ... because we're a bunch of kids."

"Just say 'excuse me' and keep on walking. Pass it down!"

Those words were repeated a few hundred times: *"Just say 'excuse me' and keep on walking. Pass it down."*

And after the word had spread, Mandalay raised her right arm and made a forward motion, like an officer leading troops into battle, and shouted "Let's Go!" and the thousands of young teens began walking slowly towards the roadblock.

Gute, with a smile on his face, scooped up Daisy and said, "This is gonna be just fine." He lowered his head and put her on his shoulders for a piggyback ride.

The SHOUTNews reporter shouted into his microphone: "I can't believe what I'm about to witness. This could be a massacre."

Major Grunsky saw them coming and raised a bullhorn to his mouth. But he hesitated. Normally, he would order his soldiers, as confrontation neared, to ready their guns.

But jeez, he couldn't say that here. These were kids, after all, carrying bottled water and granola bars.

So for the first time in his long career as a combat officer, the grizzled commander said into the bullhorn, "Ok, please, we would like you to stop. Please, please stop. Please."

He used the word *please* four times. How polite of him.

The marchers were 25 feet away. "Just say 'excuse me' and keep on walking," Mandalay, Gute and Jazmin shouted, as a reminder.

And that's exactly what they did. They sidestepped and dipped under and around the well-armed soldiers and said, "Excuse me," "Excuse me," "Excuse me" so many times they probably broke the Guinness Book of World Records, and what were the soldiers gonna do?

Not a darn thing. Mandalay was right.

After the first 100 or so kids had ducked under and around, the soldiers broke their blockade, laid down their guns and made it easier for the kids to pass. They began collecting their empty water bottles and giving them their filled canteens.

"You all will need this later, it's a hot one," one soldier said, and then soldier after soldier started handing over their canteens.

"Good luck," the soldiers started saying, and before not too long, they were exchanging high fives with the teens. Little did they know, they would meet again.

Chapter 11: Gotta pee!

BY 12:30, AFTER HAVING WALKED seven miles, the sun a blazing 99 degrees and having guzzled water bottle after water bottle, word began filtering up: "Need a break. Gotta pee."

It seemed the boys were not shy about whizzing on the side of the road in Jersey. But the girls wanted privacy.

Mandalay, Gute and Jazmin gave themselves the look: *Oohhh, we didn't think of that one, either.*

Before stopping global warming, there was the not-so-small issue of going to the bathroom.

They would have to improvise.

Gute looked at the trusty map he had brought along, because tech was taboo. They were too far away from a town with toilets.

Mandalay, once again, shouted out her message: "This is what we're gonna do. Take out your ponchos, tie them together, find sticks and make little tents for the girls in the grass on the side of the road. The girls can enter and pee. You all have toilet paper and garbage bags, so ... Please pass it down."

She didn't think she needed to spell out everything. There was a lot of giggling as the plan unfolded.

"Well, I'm not sure what's going on down there," the SHOUT-News reporter shouted into his microphone, "but it looks like all these kids are making lots and lots *and lots* of little tents ... and I'm just not sure what they're doing, but they sure look well-organized, because they're all doing the exact same thing."

The kids took this time to eat and rest. There were now about 5,000 kids marching, because hundreds and hundreds of kids from New Jersey had joined in. They must have eaten 10,000 granola bars and 10,000 bananas and drank 10,000 bottles of water in about 15 minutes. Another entry for the Guinness Book of World Records.

Within a half hour, they resumed walking.

A boy from the Jersey City Town School choir began singing John Lennon's *Imagine*. Before not too long, everyone joined in.

Because of the whirring noise from the helicopter, the SHOUTNews reporter couldn't hear a thing. But one very smart kid fixed that. She called 1-800-ShoutIt on her ring and was patched through to the chopper. Through her ring, the reporter could now hear plain and clear what was happening. He broadcast it to the world.

A choir of 5,000 singing Lennon's epic song.

SHOUTNews normally had a small number of listeners and viewers, unless huge happened: a hurricane, a horrible crime or some political fart storm.

This event was not huge yet, but it was gaining momentum.

Approximately 500,000 people were now following along with SHOUTNews as these kids marched and sang their way through Jersey, including Gertrude Johnson, who was watching the net as she enjoyed her butter cake with hot tea. She had been on the phone just that morning with grandson Billy, who had assured his grandma that he had done what she asked. In fact, Billy's girls, as Gertrude liked to call them, were watching the march on their dweeb in the girl's bathroom at school, hiding in a stall so their teachers wouldn't know. They figured the marchers would take at least two weeks to get to D.C.

By 5:30 pm, the singing had stopped and word began to spread: *exhausted, starving, hot as hot could be, need to stop for the night.*

Chapter 12: Food?

MANDALAY SAW THE EXHAUSTION AROUND her: Some kids were having difficulty lifting their legs because they were so tired. The marching had slowed to a shuffle. Everyone was soaked with sweat. Their feet stung from bloody blisters ... and walking in squishy, sweat-soaked socks felt like marching in a swamp.

They had walked 14 miles in blazing heat. An amazing, but exhausting first day. Now, the tricky part.

Finding food.

"What are we gonna do now?" Mandalay heard a girl say. "If I eat one more granola bar, I'll puke."

Mandalay felt the same way. She looked around and saw lots and lots and *lots* of very unhappy teens, moaning and dragging their feet, just trying to make it to the finish line, wherever that might be for the night. She figured they'd stop near the closest New Jersey town and all go off and buy food. Wishful thinking.

Gute took out his map, and they studied it. They were trying to find a nearby town with enough food to feed a lot of kids. That was impossible.

What they found was a large, empty field near the stinky oil refineries lining the highway. They held their noses and occupied the field. Then they mobbed the only local deli and bought out the place. But most kids got nothing.

Soon after, Jazmin heard it first, then Gute, then Mandalay. The calls home.

"Mom, I'm so hot and tired. If I don't get some food soon, I'm gonna pass out," one boy could be heard saying on his ring.

"Dad, my feet hurt so much I can't even stand up," one girl, near tears, said on her call home.

Mandalay, Gute and Jazmin saw the sad scene unfold right in front of them: Exhausted, starving, disgustingly sweaty and miserable kids, complaining on their rings to mom or dad, with the inevitable snowball effect: Dozens of calls or zaps, followed by dozens more ... *after just one day.*

Mandalay suddenly felt the pangs in her stomach, not of hunger, but of fear, fear of an early failure. Hundreds and hundreds of African butterflies had awoken, and snakes were now hissing after them.

Mandalay huddled with Gute and Jazmin.

"I feel a deluge coming on, and I don't mean a rainblast," Mandalay said, as they watched hundreds of kids making plans to go home. They began repacking their backpacks and walking to the road.

"If this is happening after just one day, can you imagine what'll happen tomorrow?" Mandalay said to Gute and Jazmin, shaking her head. "We'll end up in Washington all by ourselves."

She thought for a moment. "Ok, we may have screwed up by not planning, but how could we have planned for all these kids?" She shook her head in frustration.

"Mandalay, it doesn't matter now," Jazmin said.

"Yeah, you're right, we'll just have to deal with it," Mandalay said.

She kicked over a metal garbage can and jumped on top.

"Hey everyone, we need you to stay!" she shouted out. "We need to show the politicians in Washington ..."

Only the kids closest could hear her, because they were spread out so widely. And the truth was, most kids were too hungry and too tired to listen.

Mandalay, the ultimate optimist, was feeling desperate, looking for an answer.

"Do you see what I see?" Jazmin shouted, pointing about 30 yards downfield.

They looked, squinting in the blinding, low, early-evening sun.

"Yes!" Mandalay shouted.

It was Jonny Jackson, interviewing kids.

"Where did she come from?" Mandalay said to her friends.

The three of them raced down to greet her.

"Hey Jonny, how's it going?" an excited Mandalay said. "We're really surprised to see you here."

"I was watching SHOUT and I realized you had pulled this off. I'm really impressed. So I talked to my editor and ..."

As they were talking, a boy nearby yelled out, "Mom!" He didn't say anything else. He just picked up his backpack and ran towards her, like he was a soldier returning from war.

The mother hugged and kissed her son and they walked towards a car.

Other kids were walking to the edge of the field, expecting to be picked up.

There were more shouts of "*mom*"... "*dad.*"

"So how's it going?" Jonny asked.

"It's going great," Mandalay lied, as she steered Jonny down the field, away from the fleeing kids, but that wasn't easy, because a lot of kids were going home. "We walked 14 miles today, and breezed right through the National Guard. Did you see that on the net?"

Jonny was distracted for a second by the parade of kids leaving.

"Yeah ... uhm, you know, I'm making a live broadcast in about" – she looked at her watch – "three minutes. I was promoted to staff reporter, so I can interview you live - if you want."

Mandalay looked at Gute. They had that no-tech deal, so she couldn't do a net interview without his approval. "What do you think?" she asked him.

Gute looked at Mandalay, then at Jazmin. He was thinking it through, but not for too long. "This is an emergency, yeah - go for it."

"Ok, Jonny," Mandalay said, nodding. She took a nervous breath and got ready for her first ever live interview.

Jonny turned on her Ring-a-Ling-Ding-Ping 30ZIPX, with a micro mini-zoom lens that expanded from the ring, a special mini-camera that allowed for a live worldwide broadcast.

"Ok," Jonny said into a wireless microphone. Then she held up her ring and began broadcasting to the world.

"Good evening. As you can see, I'm here on a large field in New Jersey, with thousands of very tired kids who had an amazing day, one they won't soon forget. They're part of a march on Washington, D.C., to stop global warming. They're risking being expelled from school to well … I hate to sound overly dramatic … to help save the world."

She then faced Mandalay.

"And I'm here with the leader of this movement. Mandalay Hawk is about the toughest, most dedicated teenager you'll ever see."

It turns out *The Sunny Day News* evening broadcast had three million viewers, and Tom Hawk had turned on his dweeb. He was thrilled and relieved to see his smiling daughter on screen.

"So Mandalay," Jonny continued, "you had an eventful day. You walked a lot of miles today and I understand you faced armed soldiers on the GW Bridge. How did you get past them?"

"Well, ok … uhm," Mandalay stuttered, tongue tied for her first ever live interview. "We, uhm, yeah … well, you see, we're just a bunch of kids. So I told everyone to basically ignore them and walk through."

"And what happened?"

Mandalay nodded. "They smiled, handed us their canteens and let us pass. It was, well, what I expected."

Mandalay was gaining confidence.

"You expected that?"

"Well, yeah Jonny, you see, when kids work together, put their minds to it … Well, they really can't be stopped."

Mandalay said this despite the traffic jam on nearby roads as parents came to retrieve their kids. Jonny was aware of this.

"And Mandalay, as good a day as it was, could you use some help? I mean, you can't get to Washington all by yourselves, can you?"

Jonny was setting up Mandalay, so she could just say those

magic words to the three million people watching live: *Yes, we need help.*

But Mandalay was Mandalay. She got caught up in the moment, let her enthusiasm get the best of her. She could not ask for help. "Well, we're very confident - confident and independent," she said. "We had a great day marching today and we'll have a great day tomorrow, too." She seemed to forget all about those hungry kids going home.

But Gute and Jazmin didn't. They were watching the sorry scene unfold around them. More and more kids, exhausted and starving, were shuffling to the road, ending their march. Jazmin nodded to Gute - then walked right into Mandalay's live interview and stood next to her good friend. A surprised Mandalay glanced at Jazmin. Jonny had no choice but to introduce her.

"Ok, I see that Mandalay's friend has joined the interview. This is Jazmin Morjani, and apparently she has something to add."

"Well, yeah, while Mandalay was talking … uhmm, well, some things were happening. It turns out we don't have quite as much food as we thought. We're a bunch of young teens marching. So now we could use some help from older kids. We need food. Lot's of it."

Well, there's something about a call for help from a few thousand kids stranded on a field nearby. Jazmin made it clear they wanted help from teens only - *not adults*. The message was seen by the millions of viewers, then zapped and rezapped throughout the New Jersey high school scene - the football, basketball and soccer teams, cheerleaders, debate clubs, cooking clubs - from team to team, club to club, and school to school. Mandalay, Gute and Jazmin, who were 14, were intentionally marching only with young teens, because they are less threatening to adults. But it didn't mean they couldn't ask older kids for help.

Mandalay grudgingly understood the call for help. "Yeah, I get it. We're all really hungry," she said to Gute and Jazmin.

Within two hours, the roads around the field were jammed with cars delivering food. Hundreds of teenagers, from all over Jersey, were dropping off pizzas; bags of burgers, burritos and sandwiches; buckets of fried chicken; cartons of fruit and vegetables; loaves of bread; boxes of cookies, cakes, muffins and bagels; and case after case of bottled water and Gatorade.

"Hey, what you're doing is a really cool thing," said Derrick, a high school senior from Passaic, New Jersey, who seemed to be one of the organizers bringing in food. "You know, if you need any more help …"

"Thanks, we'll see what happens," Mandalay said, cutting him off. She didn't ask him for his phone number or zap address, because she was too caught up in the moment.

"Mom, it's ok, you can go home now," one kid from Staten Island said to his mother, as he rushed over to grab some mushroom pizza.

It was as if these kids had not eaten in a month. There was a controlled stampede, with some kids trying to organize a line, kids grabbing food and piling it six-inches high on paper plates, then sitting on the field and stuffing their faces.

"So, do you expect this to happen every night?" Jonny asked Mandalay later, as they wolfed down burritos and Gatorade. "I mean, this is pretty amazing, all these kids helping. Don't tell me you thought something like this would happen."

Mandalay was thinking, but she wasn't sure what to say. "All I know is, we'll get to DC, and we won't starve to death, Jonny, that I know," she said. "The details, well …"

Her voice trailed off. She just shrugged. She resumed eating her dinner.

Chapter 13: Expelled ... Forever!!!

MEANWHILE, BACK AT HEMINGWAY HIGH, Bushwick was finishing his paperwork for the day. He sat at his desk, with a pile of 44 neatly typed and signed letters in front of him. The three letters for Mandalay, Gute and Jazmin had the same bold, black headline on top:

EXPULSION NOTICE

For being an instigator and causing students to be absent from school on May 15, 2031, and causing them to miss the MANDATORY Tech IQ Test, you are hereby expelled from Ernest Hemingway High School. You are not permitted to enter this school again.

Signed: Homer Bushwick, Principal

Bushwick personally drafted the notice, so there would be no confusion down the road. The other 41 letters - suspension notices - were for their very foolish Hemingway classmates who followed along. Bushwick felt awfully good about this punishment because, finally, in the end, he and his brother would have Mandalay Hawk out of their lives - *forever.*

Or so he thought.

Chapter 14: Oh yeah, swimming in Jersey

T HEY ATE LEFTOVERS FOR BREAKFAST.
By 9 am, the 4,500 eager teens still left on the march, now psyched and well fed, rolled south on Interstate 95. They stuck to the right shoulder of the road, stretching back half a mile. Because of all the rubbernecking, cars and trucks drove past slowly.

Every two hours, the kids took a pee, water and snack break. They had a routine. Most dashed to the woods to take a leak. A few girls still used poncho tents, but most were less and less shy.

"New Jersey was always a smelly state," the SHOUTNews reporter told his listeners. "But now …"

He didn't need to finish his sentence. His viewers could see kids by the hundreds dashing to the woods to do their business.

And, of course, motorists had opinions.

"You kids are crazy!" more than a few yelled.

"You punks - go home, where you belong!" others screamed.

But there were supporters. "Don't give up, no matter what happens!" one lady yelled.

By noon, it was 100 degrees and it's fair to say every single kid was soaked with sweat, semi-delusional and dreaming of a nearby lake that didn't exist.

Mandalay, Gute and Jazmin realized something had to be done. The broiling sun was beating down on them, and there was no lake or ocean on the horizon for thousands of sweltering teens.

"I have an idea," Gute said, so Jazmin blew her whistle and they yelled out a 10-minute break. The three huddled over Gute's map. They knew it was five minutes to Jonny's next news update.

Jonny did not look so good herself, so Gute opened a bottle of water and poured it over her head.

"Eeechs!" Jonny yelled, as she jumped. "That felt great!"

A few minutes later, Jonny said into her microphone: "Day two, we have walked a total of 21 miles, pushing south. We've had few, if any defectors yet today, but it's steamy hot out here."

She put the microphone in Mandalay's face.

"Hi everyone," said a cheerful Mandalay, who had realized how helpful Jonny could be. "We're walking and we're broiling out here. So we thought of veering off to take a dip in the Atlantic, but that would mean a lot of extra miles."

She was trying to be cute. Gute and Jazmin rolled their eyes once again at their friend.

"So we thought perhaps someone – perhaps some firefighters who have some down time - could help us out. We're still walking to Washington without adult help, but we could use a roadside soak to help cool off."

Mandalay half smiled and hunched her shoulders, meaning *maybe ... please ... perhaps?*

This roadside soak was Gute's idea. In the middle of the day, there were only two million people watching *The Sunny Day News* netcast. But it just so happens, firefighters, as brave as they are, sometimes had breaks, waiting in their firehouses for the next emergency. This included approximately a dozen Jersey fire departments within a 10-mile radius of the marchers.

The SHOUTNews chopper saw it first: a snaking line of fire trucks heading towards the highway.

At the next exit sign in New Jersey, firefighters held up a huge handmade sign:

Want to take a dip in our lake?

That was kind of a stupid question. Kids just dropped their backpacks and ran. Thousands of kids running, as fast as they could, down the exit ramp. No one seemed to care that they were in a stinky part of Jersey, the nauseating smell of oil refineries fresh with every breath.

This also was probably another one of those historic firsts: Dozens of fire engines lined up on the side of the road, firefighters holding their hoses skyward.

The firefighters saw the mob racing towards them. A fire chief waited, then raised his arm - and shouted: "Ok, turn 'em on!"

And like magic, there was a gauntlet of cold, raining water for these overheated, sweaty kids to run and dance and hop through. Some just stood there, looked up and let the cool spray hit them in the face. Boys took off their hats and shirts and threw them in the air. No one cared that their clothes and shoes got totally soaked.

For 15 minutes these kids pranced and jumped in the water and high-fived as many firefighters as possible.

But then it was back to business.

They followed Mandalay, Gute and Jazmin back onto I-95, going south, now only about 200 miles from DC. They walked several miles and then one crazy kid yelled out: "Let's run to DC!"

The SHOUTNews reporter got another eyeful. Thousands of kids, soaked with water-logged shoes, jogging with backpacks bouncing up and down on their backs.

The jogging lasted all of five minutes, tops. Exhausted, delirious, and needing water, they all sat down and gulped.

After drinking two bottles in record time, Gute took off his shoes and socks, held up his feet and showed off his bloody blisters. He was not alone. Band-Aids were being passed up and down the line.

Day #2 was nearing its end, about 25 miles total walked so far, dinner time approaching.

Mandalay was looking for Jonny, it was about that time. She was expecting a repeat of the night before. She found Jonny walking in the middle of the pack, having a heated conversation on her ring. Jonny saw Mandalay coming and waved her off.

Jonny was speaking to her editor. No longer just a reporter in training, she felt she could speak her mind.

"That's nonsense, and you know it," Jonny said, thrusting her right hand through the air in anger. "You can't do this." She was really pissed as she clicked off her ring.

She walked over to Mandalay, shaking her head. "Sorry, my newspaper doesn't want a live report tonight. Tomorrow morning – '*If there's news to report,*' my editor said."

"I don't get it. Just a few hours ago, they wouldn't let you off the air," Mandalay said.

"Yeah, I know. Since then, my paper, supposedly, has received hundreds of complaints. *'Are we covering the news or making it?'* my editor whined. He said we need to take a break."

"That sucks," Mandalay said. "We need you to make a broadcast. We need dinner."

"I'm sorry - I can't. They won't put me on the air."

Mandalay shook her head. She looked at Gute and Jazmin, who heard what Jonny said.

The "swim" from earlier in the day had worn off hours ago and the marching teens were overheated, exhausted, thirsty, starving and looking for a Day 2 miracle.

They had marched south in Jersey, and now were heading towards a large field Gute found on the map, near the highway. A large empty field, with no food and only a few portable toilets for a nearby construction site.

As they rolled into the field, kids dumped their backpacks and ran off in search of food. They found a pizzeria. Within 15 minutes, 60 seaweed/rice pies had been ordered, but the pizzeria ran out of that yucky dough. A deli made wraps at a frantic pace, but it ran out, too. The local Chinese restaurant was overrun with so many hungry kids it offered fried rice for free. But most kids didn't get anything. There just wasn't enough food to go around.

Mandalay wished she had gotten Derrick's contact info, but she didn't.

"I have a plan," Gute said.

He looked upwards and squinted - into the hot, clear, sunny sky - and pointed.

"If you look closely, you can see them up there - *see ...* " He was pointing up, into the sky. "... the high-altitude mini-drones. They're following us. I hate tech, but this is an emergency. They're watching every move we make."

They all looked up and sure enough, there were dozens of dark specks in the sky overhead, circling like small, distant birds. A lot of kids, with their homemade drones, were following the march and watching.

"Ok, yeah, I see them. So what's the plan?" Mandalay wondered, as she gazed upward, using her hand to shield the sun from her eyes.

Mandalay, Gute and Jazmin huddled for a few minutes. Gute did most of the talking. Then they talked with some of the marchers and began shouting instructions. The message was passed down. It took about 15 minutes for the word to spread and for them to get organized, with some kids still eating mashed bananas and smashed granola bars and many others collapsed on the field from exhaustion.

Eventually, kids gathered themselves to form zig zagging lines, stepping over and around backpacks and sleeping bags strewn about. Their lines formed letters, which then formed words.

By around 6 pm, this is what all those mini-drones, and the SHOUTNews chopper saw:

NEED FOOD - AGAIN!

"The little wankers need to stop whining and just go home," the SHOUTNews reporter complained to his audience. "How many handouts can they expect?"

But many Jersey teens saw it differently. The drones captured the message and with a few toggles, the video was zapped and rezapped across Jersey. Before not too long, there was a steady stream of cars delivering food again.

The local high school kids had come through for a second night in a row, but there was a big but. All the kids got dinner, but there wasn't as much food as the night before. Just not as much interest in helping out. Mandalay took note of this and glanced at Gute and Jazmin.

"No one will get seconds tonight, that's for sure," Gute said, shaking his head.

Chapter 15: Ultra Top Secret!

MEANWHILE, NEWS OF THE MARCH was spreading around the country and the world. Even though the media was sick and tired of covering global warming, it could not ignore thousands of kids marching in broiling heat. By 9 pm that night, boosted by the drone coverage, half a dozen media helicopters with TV cameras were now circling overhead. The march was for young teens only, and they were taking note. Kids had started zapping and rezapping. The story was ping ponging across the net, and across the country.

The government's own secret satellites noticed it, too. Government officials were watching closely. They didn't like what they saw: Young teens across the country were ditching school, and telling their parents they didn't care if they got in trouble, because they had to march.

In Butte, Montana, 14 members of Mountain High's Junior Environmental Club decided to march out of the mountains and hitch a ride to DC. The JV soccer team from Pasadena High, in California, and nine members of the cooking club from Desert High in Phoenix were heading east. The JV track team from Ocean High in Fort Lauderdale, to stay in shape, was bicycling north. A dozen eighth, ninth and tenth graders from Parish Middle-High in New Orleans, and thousands more from all over the country were on their way. Walking, biking, hitching – whatever it took. The government was getting nervous.

"We have to watch this closely," Vice President Chung instructed General Wildegard, the chairman of the Joint Chiefs of Staff. "The president has far more important things on his mind than worrying about a bunch of bratty teens. We must deal with global warming our way. If word goes virile and we lose control, it could start a dangerous, national stampede of kids towards Washington. We have to contain and control these kids." There was a meeting in the War Room in the Pentagon.

ULTRA TOP SECRET MEMORANDUM:

U.S. Government's Plan to End March on Washington, D.C.

Let them march. Let them get totally, totally, totally exhausted and so hot, sweaty and disgustingly filthy after walking all those miles they can't take it anymore. Attrition will mount as the exhaustion, heat and hunger takes its toll. Broiling temps are working in our favor. They have a Constitutional right to march and assemble and the right of free speech, so we will not impede the march. But the march will implode. We expect to wrap this up pronto.

Signed: *General Hampton Henry Humboldt Wildegard III, Chairman, Joint Chiefs of Staff*

Chapter 16: Reality check - Mandalay's Dilemma, #2

I T WAS ABOUT 10 PM, dark, still and hot. There was virtual silence. Kids were not laughing or singing or throwing Frisbees or doing anything. There was no music, no talking, no nothing.

Mandalay sat in the middle of the field leaning against her backpack. She looked around. Boys were shirtless, girls wore shorts and tank tops. They were all sprawled on top of their sleeping bags, some still with their shoes on, too tired to take them off.

Mandalay expected at least a little fun - laughing, singing, goofing around ... something.

But no. Everyone, including Gute and Jazmin, was fast asleep.

A sea of thousands of kids conked out on a giant field in Jersey.

If these kids were this exhausted after day 2, what would they be like after day 5? After day 10?

There also was that constant trickle of attrition. Enough exhausted and overheated kids had whined to their mom and dad on their rings that now about 750 kids had gone home.

And the food for dinner - about half what was delivered the first night.

Mandalay was now thinking – *really thinking* – about something she and her friends had avoided, dodged and ducked for months: *Good ole food and mileage.*

As the days ticked by, how much food and water could they really expect to have delivered each night? And how many miles a day could they actually walk?

Day 1: 14 miles. A very good start.

Day 2: 11 miles. Not as good, but not bad.

Day 3: *A big, fat question mark?*

What about days 4 and 5?

These were the details Mandalay and her friends had avoided like a nest of scorpions on a hot desert hike, but now they were flooding her mind, drowning the adrenalin rush of taking Washington by storm. Mandalay sat on the grass, her legs bent in front of her, her arms resting on her knees.

She was finally thinking it through: *It was not realistic to think they could walk to Washington, certainly not in this heat. It never was realistic.* But she wouldn't dare let herself ever think that thought.

They were heading south. The weather report: unrelenting, unforgiving, blasting, broiling heat. Over 100 degrees every day for the next week. Baghdad in Jersey.

Even if every fire department came out to soak them, they still ...

Mandalay was shaking her head.

If they walked 10 miles a day, it would take them 20 more days.

What if they couldn't even walk 10 miles a day?

And what if the food stopped coming? What if ...?

Never once in her life had Mandalay let a dilemma – *and this was a whopper of a dilemma* – overwhelm her, dominate her, defeat her. But this truly was Mandalay's dilemma.

She thought about the Big Shaboozle and Judge Baxter. And the nasty Bushwick brothers. She had overcome them, but now ...

A sense of desperation was setting in.

But no, she could overcome ...

But no, this problem *was* insurmountable ...

But no, no, *it wasn't*. They'd figure it out, *right?*

Mandalay wasn't sure what to think ... *or do.*

She actually felt weak herself. She had dropped several pounds in two days of marching and sweating.

Her eyelids grew heavy. She felt a sudden wave of heat roll through her body, a relaxed sensation, from head to toe. Her seated body tilted forward, her head drooped and she fell slowly to the right, her head landing gently on top of her sleeping bag. She had fallen asleep.

Chapter 17: Too Hot to Handle!

O N THE THIRD DAY, THEY began marching by eight. By 10 am it was 95, by 11 it was 99. By 11:50, it hit 104 degrees. Kids at first started getting headaches. Then three fainted within a span of five minutes.

Mandalay's bad feeling from the night before got worse as she saw what was happening.

"Ok, anyone who is not feeling well needs to get in the shade!" Mandalay yelled. "Make those poncho tents to cool kids off! Pass it down!"

The kids went to work to help each other out. Of course, not only were all those mini-drones and news choppers watching, but so was the government, aware of the weather report, aware of the danger of marching in extreme heat.

Vice President Chung had been watching the government's satellite feed with the secretary of homeland security and the attorney general. Once the first kids went down, the VP gave Gen. Wildegard an order: "Send in the national guard and make sure these kids are ok. We can't have them getting sick and dying on the side of the road. The world is watching."

And indeed, the world was watching, with all those cameras in the sky, a lot like vultures circling overhead.

So this is what happened: Upon Gen. Wildegard's order, five hundred members of the New Jersey National Guard, who had been on high alert since the incident on the GW Bridge, sped to the scene. Ten specially-equipped, air-conditioned medical trucks were brought in.

A new, tougher officer was put in charge. Colonel Brenda Barksdale, a middle-aged woman with short hair and posture so straight she appeared to be about six and a half feet tall, had fought in the wars in Iraq, Afghanistan and Saudi Arabia and was used to giving orders.

But Mandalay was not used to taking them.

"I'm sorry, but I'm going to have to call off the march for today," Colonel Barksdale told Mandalay, as she stood ram-rod straight surrounded by her armed soldiers. "I've been ordered to stop you if there is a heat emergency. And, young lady, this is a heat emergency."

Behind her, soldiers were carrying kids on stretchers to air conditioned trucks.

Colonel Barksdale offered Mandalay her canteen. But Mandalay hated the government's order - and hated being called *young lady*.

"I don't need your water, or your help," Mandalay huffed, motioning to the medical scene behind her. "We'll be ok."

Mandalay turned to her friends. "If we stop now, our march is dead. We might as well just start chanting *Long Live Global Warming.*" She shook her head in frustration.

Gute and Jazmin had heard the colonel. They understood the dilemma.

"We need to take a break," Jazmin said to Mandalay and Gute. "It's too dangerous to march right now." She looked at Gute for back up.

"Yeah, I agree," he said, looking worried as the soldiers carried more kids past them on stretchers to the medical trucks. "We need to be patient."

Mandalay saw the scene around her. She was not happy. She began pacing.

"I don't want anyone to get sick, but we can't stay here forever," she said. She thought of the dilemma that ran through her mind the night before.

Mandalay turned to Colonel Barksdale and said: "We just need to rest for a few minutes. I understand a few kids can't make it."

"Young lady," Colonel Barksdale said sternly, sounding way too much like a school principal or parent, repeating those two words Mandalay hated to hear. "This is not just about a few kids. This is a medical emergency. I've just been informed we now have 53 kids in the medical trucks with early-stage heat stroke. They'll be fine. But some kids will not be fine if you keep marching.

"Let me be frank and honest with you, Mandalay Hawk: I know all about you. I know where you're from and what you're about. You defy authority at all costs. In the military, you don't defy authority. Kids will die if you keep marching. So I'm shutting you down for today."

"No you're not," Mandalay shot back. "Those of us who can march have the right to continue. You can't stop us!"

"Yes, I can!" Colonel Barksdale shouted back. And with those words, Colonel Barksdale spoke into her high-powered military ring: "Impose the road block. And this time, I don't want to see kids walking past soldiers."

They had walked four, slow miles.

The kids were so hot and tired they didn't even challenge the soldiers or bother to walk off the highway. They just lay down in the grass on the side of the road. Soldiers pitched large tents with open sides so the kids could get out of the sun.

At 2 pm, local fire departments, after hearing the news, sent trucks to give them a much needed sprinkle.

But Mandalay knew they needed a lot more than tents and water to get through this.

Chapter 18: "General, we have a problem ..." (aka, Mandalay's Dilemma, #2, continued)

M ANDALAY LOOKED AT HER WATCH. It was 3 pm on May 17, 2031. She looked up, and saw all those drones and whirling helicopters, and knew there were invisible government satellites in the sky as well, all watching and broadcasting their march to the world. She knew what failure would signal to everyone: *Kids can't stop global warming - now or ever.*

"We're doing the right thing by walking to Washington, but we need to deal with reality," Gute said to Mandalay and Jazmin. "It's freakin' hot out here."

"Yeah, I know, but it doesn't mean we can't march," Mandalay said. "We can all push through this heat if we put our minds to it."

Jazmin looked at her friend in disbelief and shook her head.

"You are one stubborn girl," Jazmin said angrily. "Did you hear what that officer said? Kids will *die* if we keep marching."

"Sorry Gute, but I need to show this to our leader." Jazmin held up her forbidden ring and tapped on the weather app. The ring's screen displayed the weather report for the next five days.

"Take a look, sweetheart," Jazmin huffed to Mandalay. The entire report was scarlet red. The app reserved that color for extreme weather, like hurricanes, rainbombs, Hail from Hell or what was coming: *Extreme, blasting, scorching, life-threatening heat.*

109

110

111

114

117

"This makes that hail storm look like a light drizzle," Jazmin said.

Mandalay looked at her friends, then at the scene around her, a few thousand kids lying under large army tents, too hot to move.

She looked at the flow of traffic on the highway, all those rubbernecking gawkers, all those sucky adults thinking these kids had failed.

They couldn't possibly fight global warming, because they can't even get out of Jersey.

Off in the distance, Mandalay could see the New York City skyline. She shook her head in frustration. She was awfully pissed. For the first time, a nasty thought shot through her mind: *that they had been set up – set up to fail by the weather, by the sucky adults of the world and by the sucky government, in a twisted, demented conspiracy to keep global warming cooking. And, eventually, all of them will get scorched, with the world watching.*

She took another deep breath, and thought some more - and tried to think through the problem.

No … no … no, that can't really happen, she thought. *No - no way.*

She now realized, finally, after three days of marching and seeing all these kids get sick, that they had no choice. They would need help getting to Washington.

"We need a plan to get out of here - *now*," she said to Gute and Jazmin. For 30 seconds, Mandalay stood there, on the side of the highway, with a sea of hot and exhausted kids lying around her, trying to think through this dilemma. She saw dozens of cars pass them on the highway, some whose occupants yelled out to them. She realized most of the supportive comments were coming from young people.

"Keep going, save the world!" one girl shouted as she drove by with a friend in a red sports car.

"We're counting on you!" a boy shouted, from the back of a pickup truck.

Mandalay listened, thought, and then nodded - because something clicked. "Okay," she said to Gute and Jazmin. "I got an idea." The three huddled once again. Mandalay explained what she had in mind.

"Ok, we can give it a try," Gute said. "Anything to get out of the sun."

"Yeah," Jazmin agreed, nodding. They passed down a message.

Within 15 minutes, the drivers passing all those kids on the side of the road, and all those eyes in the sky, saw kids forming zig zagging lines, which created the following message:

Need a ride to Washington from YOUNG PEOPLE – NOW!!!

Colonel Barksdale rushed over with armed soldiers.

"Stop this nonsense!" she commanded Mandalay, who was in the middle of the message.

Mandalay actually laughed at this tall and tough colonel.

"Sorry, this ain't nonsense and we ain't stopping for you or anyone else," Mandalay said, smiling. "We know our First Amendment rights and we know you're not allowed to touch us - so don't even try."

And the world stood as witness. Jonny's camera was rolling, as were cameras from all those drones, choppers and satellites.

The message stayed put – and what happened is just what Mandalay hoped for. Word zapped and rezapped like a spreading wildfire among young people, who love road trips the way a five-year old loves lollipops.

Barksdale and her soldiers stood and watched. They couldn't do a thing.

Hundreds and hundreds of high school juniors and seniors with freshly minted licenses and college kids from nearby schools rolled in. Within two hours, 4,000-plus kids were stuffed into every kind of car imaginable - SUVs, sedans, sports cars, vans, pickup trucks, electric and gas guzzling - you name it - and were on their way south to Washington, D.C. Mandalay, Gute and Jazmin agreed that no driver could be over the age of 23.

"General, we have a problem," an exasperated Colonel Barksdale said to General Wildegard on her military ring. "These kids are heading to Washington."

The SHOUTNews reporter couldn't believe what he was seeing. "How can this be?" he said in disbelief, as car after car headed south.

"Well, Washington, you better get ready, because some knowledgeable and eager kids are heading your way," Jonny Jackson said into the microphone, pleased *The Sunny Day News* had finally put her back on the air. "Word has it, they're headed straight for the Lincoln Memorial."

Sara and Bergen were watching on their dweeb during lunch. They didn't expect them so soon. They made quick plans with Billy to sneak out of school early through the back door.

Chapter 19: GYBOOTN!!!
and the girls

THE GOVERNMENT HAD MORE THAN just Mandalay Hawk and her marchers to worry about. There also, now, were thousands of other kids marching towards Washington from all over the U.S.

As word spread, kids from all 49 states – *that's right, all 49 states, except for Hawaii* - began walking, hitching and biking in small groups towards Washington – on country roads, suburban streets, interstate highways. Some of them had hundreds of miles to go, some had thousands. After they got word about the hitch-hiking, they began zapping to do the same thing.

It turns out kids love to help kids, if there's a good reason.

The government was still watching - and getting more and more worried.

"I don't like this, I don't like this one bit," the FBI director said to the vice president, as they watched their secret satellite feed and saw more and more kids heading towards DC.

It was just after 5 o'clock in the morning in Beijing, where President Billingham was fast asleep in the U.S. embassy. He was there on an important diplomatic trip.

An aide entered the president's bedroom, walked over to his bed, and as he was instructed to do, tapped the president's shoulder and said, "Mr. President, you have an urgent call from the states."

"What?" the groggy president mumbled.

"You have an urgent call, Mr. President," the aide repeated.

"Uhhh," the president grunted, as he sat up and clicked on the light. He shook his head in disgust.

The president picked up the secure phone next to his bed.

"Yes," President Billigham answered.

"Hi, dad," his two girls said simultaneously. "How's it going?"

President Billingham looked at his aide quizzically - *This is urgent?*

"Everything okay? Is mommy alright?" he asked.

"Well, yeah dad, everything's fine," said Sara.

"Well then, you know I love you, but did you really need to wake me up in the middle of the night, and does mommy know you're doing this?"

The president looked at the clock. It was 5:11 am.

"Well, dad, we have something important to talk to you about," explained Sara. "You need to come home now."

The president sat up straight, glanced at his aide, then tried to act as presidential as possible.

"You know, sweethearts, I'm on an important trip and …"

"It's just that, well, there is an urgent matter developing here," Bergen interrupted. "We need you."

Almost as if on cue, a second aide rushed in. The president looked up.

"Mr. President, the FBI director and the vice president just called," the second aide said. "They said there's an urgent matter developing in the U.S."

The Secret Service has a code name for what happened next: It's called the Rapid-Departure Plan, aka RDP, also known as GYBOOTN!!!, aka *Get Your Butt Out Of Town - Now!!!*

The second aide took the phone from the president and hung it up. President Billingham didn't even get a chance to say goodbye to his girls.

The president's chief of staff told the lead secret service agent that GYBOOTN!!! was being deployed.

The president didn't have time to shave, shower or get dressed. He put on his slippers, put his coat on over his PJs, and, surrounded by Secret Service agents, walked out the door. Within 15 minutes, his motorcade delivered him to Air Force One. Within 20 minutes, he was in the air, flying east to the United States.

Once in the air, President Billingham settled into his leather command chair and had a secure video conference call with Vice President Chung and FBI Director Alhambra.

"Mr. President, something is developing here in the U.S. and we think it will require your immediate, hands-on attention," the vice president began, explaining what was happening.

"Well, they're just kids for God's sake. Let them hang in DC for a few days," was President Billingham's first reaction. "They'll be hot and exhausted. They'll get homesick and bored. They'll just want to go home."

"But Mr. President, you should be aware that their leader is this kid named Mandalay Hawk," FBI Director Alhambra explained. "She's an unusually dangerous teenage girl. She's a juvenile delinquent, who's not afraid to thwart authority and the law. I spoke to a Judge Baxter, who could have locked her up. She said: 'She's clever. She's crafty. She's dangerous. God help anyone standing in her way. *God help them.*' Those were her exact words."

"And Mr. President," Vice President Chung added. "I have to remind you that when you run for re-election, we'll need the coal and oil companies and all their billions of dollars on our side. If we take any action remotely cutting into their profits, they'll turn on us like a pack of hound dogs chasing a skunk in the woods. It will be nasty, sir."

President Billingham was thinking. *He did want to get re-elected. He loved the job - and the perks.*

"I understand," the president said. "We'll deal with this the moment I return ..."

Just then that first aide burst into the cabin.

"Mr. President, you have an urgent call on video line 2. It's your daughters."

The president sighed. He shook his head.

He loved his darlings, really loved them, but sometimes ...

He tapped line 2. Bergen and Sara appeared on screen.

"Yes, sweethearts," the president sighed.

"Dad, remember when you became president you gave us one free pass to occupy and engage you in the Oval Office on a matter of major national importance? Do you remember that, dad?" Sara asked.

The president did not remember this. He struggled to recall. "Well …"

"Well, you did dad, and here's the letter," Sara said.

Bergen waved it in the air, then added: "Dad, notice it's hand-written on White House stationary. It says right here." She pointed to the words on the letter and read:

> *Dear Sara and Bergen: I love you girls very much. During my presidency, this secret pass allows you one special trip to the Oval Office to engage me in a matter of national significance. Ice cream will be served. Love, daddy*

"Dad, we'll be occupying the Oval Office," Sara said. "We'll be waiting for you when you return. And BTW, which means *By The Way*, tell the veep and her little minions to stay out of our way. If they bother us, well, they'll see a double hissy fit the likes they've never seen before."

The girls had intentionally left the bedroom door ajar so that Billy Johnson could hear their side of the conversation. He heard it all, although he pretended not to be paying attention. He knew his grandma would be proud of him. He also knew his work was not done.

Mandalay had zapped Billy - she told Gute she had no choice. She had learned a valuable lesson the last few days: that some-times, really desperate times calls for really desperate action. Billy connected Mandalay with Bergen and Sara.

Chapter 20: The government gets tough (aka, Mandalay's Dilemma, #3)

B Y NEXT MORNING THERE WAS an historic scene. Virtually every speck of grass surrounding the Lincoln Memorial and all the stone steps leading up to it were covered in sleeping kids. They were filthy and hot, hungry and tired, but somehow these thousands of kids, led by Mandalay, Gute and Jazmin, had marched and hitchhiked their way to this sacred spot.

Colonel Barksdale and her troops were on scene. She was furious with Mandalay, but she was ordered to provide breakfast for all those kids.

The order from General Wildegard was simple: "These kids cannot go hungry. Feed and water them."

The colonel talked to the captain, who talked to the lieutenant, who whispered to the master sergeant in charge of the kitchen. Ok, if we have to give 'em breakfast, well, *give 'em breakfast*.

The kids woke up at 6 am to an already blistering day – it was 96, going up to 112, with Washington's sauna-like humidity. The heat did not bother Mandalay. She felt she was living her dream.

Because there she was, among 4,000 strong, in the nation's capital, lying alongside the reflecting pool, in front of the Lincoln Memorial. Mandalay looked up from her sleeping bag and saw the grand white marble house where Lincoln sat. A chill ran up and down her spine.

Despite the heat and the government's efforts to stop them, they had made it.

Mandalay recalled the photos of Dr. Martin Luther King Jr.'s historic day in 1963, when he delivered his "I have a Dream" speech from the steps of the Lincoln Memorial, to hundreds of thousands of people ... and those magical words.

I have a Dream ...

Those words that shook the nation and still rang true in 2031.

Mandalay could smell breakfast being cooked by the soldiers on the lawn on the other side of the Reflecting Pool. *Yeah, how cool was that?* Mandalay thought. *Breakfast at the Lincoln Memorial.*

"You ready?" was the good morning from Gute, with Jazmin by his side. Gute and Jazmin had unusually serious looks on their faces. They were tired, but psyched.

"Yeah, I'm ready," Mandalay said.

"Because once we eat, we have to get started. Jonny will broadcast live," Jazmin said.

Everyone was lining up for breakfast. It took only a few bites from the first few kids to realize something was wrong.

"Echh, disgusting!" a boy from Brooklyn with a ponytail yelled. He spit out some scrambled eggs on the grass.

"Oh God, too sweet, yucchh!" a girl from Queens shouted, after taking a spoonful of oatmeal. And so it went, kid after kid spitting out breakfast all over the grass. Most just spit it out and went hungry, but a few kids were so hungry they ate too much and actually puked it up.

The killer for Mandalay and her friends was when they saw Daisy throwing up in the grass, a stone's throw from the Lincoln Memorial. That's right, little 11-year-old Daisy, who had made it all the way to DC. She never called home to complain, was a tough little girl marching through the heat, even made some friends. And then this disgusting breakfast prepared by the U.S. Army made her sick.

Mandalay, Gute and Jazmin did their own taste test, and then spit it out. And then they went looking for Colonel Barksdale. She was sitting with the captain and the lieutenant eating their own breakfast, apparently a batch not seasoned with too much salt or sugar.

"What you just did was wrong!" said a furious Mandalay. "You might want to watch *The Sunny Day News* broadcast this morning. And PS – you shouldn't have just made a little girl barf up breakfast."

Perhaps this was good for Mandalay. The angrier she was, the sharper her focus.

Jonny, the 22-year-old rookie reporter, was now standing on the steps of the Lincoln Memorial, her Ring-a-Ling-Ding-Ping ready to go. She was preparing to report from one of the most hallowed spots in America. And she was pissed off - because she was really, really hungry and now had no decent breakfast to eat.

"It's hard to tell who is conspiring with whom," Jonny began, in a promo broadcast. "Yesterday, the government tried to restrain these teenagers. This morning, the government served a breakfast not fit for a dog. Are the president, the army and the big energy companies conspiring to bring these kids down? Are they trying to defeat any attempt to stop global warming? How idiotic can our government be? Tune in at 9 o'clock this morning to hear Mandalay Hawk and ..."

Her broadcast went dead.

Tom Hawk had been watching when his dweeb screen went black.

So had Gertrude Johnson, Principal Bushwick, Mr. Harkness and Judge Baxter and the 20 million other viewers now following this unfolding episode in history.

"If the crappy breakfast doesn't stop them, then cut them off if you have to," Vice President Chung ordered the FBI director and the Pentagon, after realizing that the president's re-election hung in the balance. If the president pissed off the large energy companies – the coal companies, which had made a comeback under the recent president; the natural gas companies, which were drilling like crazy; and the oil companies, which were now thriving with gas selling at $10 a gallon – he would lose.

So the FBI, the CIA and the National Security Agency blocked Jonny's transmission signal with electronic interference. And the government blocked all other media from flying overhead or from entering the area. Jonny and Mandalay could talk all they wanted, but no one in the world would hear or see them.

Chapter 21: *"Four score and seven years ago..."*

"GOSH DARN IT," MANDALAY SAID. "They're not going to stop us."

She didn't have a bull horn, but she did have strong lungs and a body, mind and soul now extra, extra full of pissed off. She knew she would have to shout out her message, because they never planned for a loudspeaker system, and hoped that her words, somehow, spread beyond DC. And she also knew they were there for the long haul, because they weren't going anywhere until they got what they wanted.

It was still a few minutes before nine, so for inspiration, she climbed up the stone steps and into the Lincoln Memorial. She stared at the grand, marble statue. It gave her goosebumps. She read the Gettysburg Address, carved in the wall:

> *Four score and seven years ago our fathers brought forth on this continent, a new nation, conceived in Liberty, and dedicated to the proposition that all men are created equal ...*

If Lincoln was alive today, he would change those last few words, Mandalay knew he would: *All men and women, all boys and girls, are created equal.*

This current government was not honoring that pledge. They were treating her and her fellow marchers like third class citizens, denying them their right to free speech and assembly.

She was getting angrier by the second.

So was Lincoln, she surmised, *his intense gaze looking out, observ-*

ing everything unfolding in front of him, sitting in moral judgment, and disapproving of the government's actions.

Mandalay drew strength from this. She sat down on the cool marble floor, pulled out her notebook and studied her notes for one last time. And when she was done, she glanced at her bracelet, the silver bracelet her dad had given her. She ran her fingers over the shiny metal.

Dad, she said to herself, *I'm not going to give up for anything. No way.*

Meanwhile, the sleepy, Saturday streets of Washington, D.C., were coming alive. What began as a trickle quickly became a steady stream, then a wide river of young teens marching and biking towards the Lincoln Memorial. Many of those kids, from states closest to DC, had hitched rides to Washington. Mandalay had expected to speak to about 4,000 kids. Now, it would be more like 25,000.

Chapter 22: "I'm 14 - You can't touch me!"

DURING HIS FLIGHT HOME FROM China, President Billingham had a secure video conference call with the CEOs of the six largest coal, oil and gas companies in the United States, companies that were planning on donating millions of dollars to his re-election campaign.

"I assure you that we have everything well under control, and this teen movement will be squashed like an ant under a boot heel," President Billingham told them.

As he said this, Sara and Bergen were walking down the hall to the Oval Office. They had a case of bottled water, a one-pound bag of M&Ms, a huge bag of potato chips - and that letter.

They arrived at the Oval Office, trailed by Billy Johnson.

"Hi girls, your dad is not back yet," the Secret Service guard at the door said.

"Yes, we know, but please move aside and let us in," said Sara.

The guard smiled. "I'll be happy to let you in once your dad is here, but I'm not authorized to …"

Bergen shoved the letter in his face. "This authorizes us to enter."

He took the letter. As he was reading, the girls pushed by him and entered the Oval Office.

"Hey!" he shouted, as they shut the door in his face and locked it.

Billy Johnson just shrugged and shook his head. "Well, they have that letter."

Mandalay was standing on the stone steps of the Lincoln Memorial, looking out at the thousands of kids on the steps and in front of the Reflecting Pool. She held a stack of papers in her hand.

Jonny's broadcast was still blocked. Mandalay was prepared to shout out her lungs. But that would not be necessary, because after talking Gute into another tech compromise, Jazmin, Gute and Jonny designed a simple communications plan.

"We're all going to link our rings to Mandalay's ring through zipzapexpress," Jazmin shouted out. "Once you link to Mandalay, then link to all your contacts. Now pass the message down."

It took a few minutes for the word to spread across the thousands of kids at the Lincoln Memorial, but now everyone's rings were linked for a common cause. They would all hear Mandalay talk, and their friends around the country could see and hear her as well through zipzapexpress.

Mandalay took a deep breath and glanced at her notes. Then she looked up at the large crowd in front of her.

"Well, finally, here we are!" she said, looking at and speaking into her ring so that her voice and image zipzapped out to everyone.

She took a deep breath to calm herself. "All of us, just a bunch of teenagers! Thousands of us from all over the country! No adults – just us!"

She paused and looked around at the throng.

"Go Mandalay!" one kid yelled.

She smiled and nodded. Although the government had banned all media helicopters and private drones overhead, the government was still watching via satellite.

"Our schools and the government have tried to stop us," Mandalay said. "They tried to flunk us out of school … They tried to block us on the GW bridge … They tried to silence us … And they tried to make us sick this morning … But they can't stop us!"

"No Way!" another kid yelled out.

"That's right, *No Way!*" Mandalay shouted back. "Because this is way too important! The world has to hear us! Did you know that the U.S. government has known since the late 1980s – *for more than 40 years* – that man-made climate change was a great danger to earth and that it had to be stopped? Did you know that?!"

Vice President Chung, the entire cabinet, the military's top generals, and the directors of the FBI, CIA and National Security Agency were packed into the Situation Room watching Mandalay via satellite.

"Where's the president? Can't we stop her?" Vice President Chung said to anyone who would listen.

Mandalay continued: "So, the U.S. and most countries in the world signed treaties vowing to cut carbon emissions so that climate change and global warming would be slowed down, put under control … and for a few years, there was progress, it looked like there was a good chance this would happen.

"And then things went backwards, forwards, sideways, then backwards again. Politicians tore up treaties. Scientific evidence was ignored and kids who protested before us didn't get the results they wanted - because politicians and adults didn't believe the problem was a true emergency. Well, they were wrong."

Mandalay looked up towards the sun.

"It's 10 o'clock in the morning and it's now over 100 degrees. This is the 9th day in a row it will hit triple digits in Washington. It was 111 in New Orleans yesterday, 113 in St. Louis, 115 in Los Angeles and 129 in Palm Springs, California. That's just in the United States. And it's May, not even summer yet.

"The average high temperature in Baghdad this month is 123 degrees. Yes, *123*. It's so hot in the Middle East and parts of Africa, India and Europe that heat stroke has become one of the leading causes of death. Thousands and thousands of people are dying because of this excessive heat.

"Now, my good friend Jazmin will tell us about the ripple effect of global warming."

"Hi everyone!" Jazmin shouted enthusiastically into her ring, as her words were zipzapped to everyone. "Great to see you all. I'm here to give you all the bad news. All these carbon emissions are having a terrible ripple effect all around the world. First of all, they cause oceans to heat up at an alarming rate. And as this has happened, the ice sheets in Greenland and Antarctica – these are the world's largest glaciers – are melting away because of the warmer temperatures. The warmer water and the ice melt have caused sea levels to rise at a life-threatening rate. The rising sea levels have caused flooding not only in the United States, but in coastal areas worldwide. The flooding, in some cases caused by extreme storms, which also are caused by global warming, has pushed hundreds of millions of people – that's right, hundreds of millions - out of their homes. They are climate-change refugees. We have thousands and thousands in New York City.

"Climate change has caused droughts. Droughts lead to food shortages and forest fires. There have been food riots all across Africa, the Middle East and parts of South America this year because millions are starving and thousands are dying. We'll have food shortages in the U.S. soon. And so much land is burning in forest fires around the United States that millions have to wear masks - and this isn't because of a pandemic.

"This has to stop!" Jazmin shouted.

Gute stepped forward. He hesitated and frowned when Jazmin handed him her ring, but he had no choice. "Did you know that this extreme heat, and its consequences, is an incubator for disease: More people will die of malaria. Millions more may die of dengue fever. And there are fears of another global pandemic. And all these problems - food shortages and disease - impact children more than adults, because a child's body is still developing, still growing.

"Yeah - as Jazmin said: *This has to stop!*" he shouted.

The crowd surrounding Gute, Jazmin and Mandalay was increasing as more and more kids arrived. The effort by the government to block the broadcast had failed miserably. The zipzap-express feed was now being picked up by the national net and was reaching a widening audience of millions.

"We can't live like this anymore!" Gute shouted again to the crowd.

"No we can't!" Mandalay shouted, as she stepped forward,

nodding to Gute and Jazmin. "So on this day, we're going to set forth our demands. These are not proposals, not requests – these are *demands*. And we're not going to leave Washington until these demands are met."

President Billingham was watching these kids via satellite feed on Air Force One. He did not like what he was hearing.

"Mr. President, I would like the authority to take drastic, non-lethal action, sir," Vice President Chung said into a secure video call to the plane.

President Billingham, thinking, took a long, deep breath.

"Sir, I guarantee it will be non-lethal," the vice president assured. "Not one kid will get hurt. But we must stop them."

President Billingham took another deep breath. He believed in free speech. But these kids were threatening his re-election.

"Ok, do what you have to do. But I don't want even one kid to get a bloody nose, understand?"

"Yes, sir."

It had hit 104 degrees and it was going up. One could reasonably argue that it was a severe health hazard for thousands of kids to be out in the broiling sun all day, with not enough water and food.

Thousands and thousands of extra National Guard soldiers had been secretly trucked in. Colonel Barksdale, surrounded by heavily armed soldiers, entered the large crowd and walked up the steps of the Lincoln Memorial towards Mandalay, Gute and Jazmin. Barksdale, sweaty, hot and angry, gave the three of them a nasty glare before she raised her bullhorn to her mouth and shouted:

"Under Washington, D.C., Health Code Section 102.978 (d) (e) (2) (i), the United States government has authority to take whatever appropriate action it deems necessary if the government believes the health and safety of individuals are at risk due to extreme weather conditions. This heat is extreme weather and we believe the health and safety of all of you are at risk."

"You already tried that yesterday!" Mandalay shouted back. "We're not going anywhere."

Barksdale's lips curled, her face tensed and her eyes narrowed. "Mandalay Hawk - that was yesterday. You were in New Jersey. Today, you're in our nation's capital. The capital of these *United! States! Of America!* Different place, different rules. You're going home!"

Then Colonel Barksdale raised her ring to her mouth and shouted: "Ok, move in!"

And then Mandalay, Gute and Jazmin and the 25,000 kids surrounding them saw something they could not believe. Thousands upon thousands of national guard soldiers emerging from cover and sprinting towards them and hundreds and hundreds of buses rushing in - all there to take these kids home. By gentle force, if necessary.

Mandalay saw this scene unfolding and knew - *knew* - it was now or never. She looked at her friends - thought for a few seconds ... then a few more. Then she shouted into her ring: "Ok, don't panic! Lie down and grab the kid's ankles in front of you. Lock bodies, squeeze tight, hold on and shout these words: *'I'm 14 - you can't touch me! I'm 14 - you can't touch me!'* Keep shouting those words - and keep your rings on."

It didn't matter that some kids were a year or two younger or older, the point was clear: *I'm a kid, you can't touch me.*

This scene was zipzappedexpressed via all those rings around the globe to a worldwide audience. And this is what the world saw: 25,000 young teens lying on the steps and the grass in front of the Lincoln Memorial, holding each other's ankles, and shouting:

I'm 14 - You can't touch me!

I'm 14 - You can't touch me!

I'm 14 - You can't touch me!

Mandalay had one more thing to do before grabbing an ankle and holding on for dear life: She zapped Bergen and Sara a one-word message: *now*

The sisters were well aware of what was going on, as they were watching the satellite feed in the Oval Office.

Four soldiers tried to pick up Mandalay. She was part of a human chain with Gute, Jazmin and a half dozen other kids, all lying on their stomachs - with Mandalay holding Gute's ankles, Jazmin holding Mandalay's ankles and on and on, kids linked to kids. When four soldiers tried to lift Mandalay, they risked busted eardrums ... because everyone around her started shouting as loud as they could:

She's 14 - You can't touch her!!!

She's 14 - You can't touch her!!!

She's 14 - You can't touch her!!!

And Mandalay closed her eyes and squeezed Gute's ankles as tight as she could, even as her face scraped the stone steps she was lying on. Mandalay turned her head and did her own screaming:

I'm 14 - You can't touch me!!!

I'm 14 - You can't touch me!!!

I'm 14 - You can't touch me!!!

As Mandalay and her friends held tight and Colonel Barksdale tried to figure out what to do, President Billingham's plane landed and he took the short ride in the Marine chopper to the White House. Within minutes he entered the Oval Office.

"Girls, it's great to see you," were the first words out of the president's mouth, trying to play nicey-nice with his daughters, knowing they were about to slam him.

"*Dad - no way!*" Sara shouted. The girls were watching the scene at the Lincoln Memorial. Mandalay and her friends had held on.

"Girls, if I don't stop this movement now, I'll be out of the White House so fast you won't have time to pack your bags," the president said.

His two daughters were angrier than he had ever seen them.

They were standing in the middle of the Oval Office, between that famous and beautiful carved wooden desk used by presidents past and present and the soft, cushy chairs and couches where world leaders often sat with the president. Their arms were crossed, their scowls were on, and they were not moving.

After a good solid minute of staring, Sara said: "Dad, this is not going to fly."

Bergen was shaking her head. "No, dad, it's not."

Bergen brought her ring up to her mouth and said: "Ok, all set."

Mandalay, Bergen and Sara had hooked their rings, so Mandalay heard Bergen's message.

Mandalay pressed the zipzapexpress button on her ring and shouted: "Now, everyone - get up, grab your backpacks and run to the White House. *Now!*"

So, with the soldiers waiting for orders, 25,000 kids in unison stood up and bolted for the White House.

"If one soldier touches one kid, what do you think the world will say?" Sara said to her dad, as they watched the satellite image of the kids tearing down the street. "Better leave them alone."

Within a half hour, the White House was surrounded by all those thousands of kids – on Pennsylvania Avenue and adjacent streets. And it only took about a minute for the chanting to start and pick up steam:

Stop Global Warming!

Stop Global Warming!!

Stop Global Warming!!!

Stop Global Warming!!!!

President Billingham stood in the middle of the Oval Office, sweating bullets, shaking his head.

Then Mandalay lifted her ring to her mouth and said: "We're coming in."

Bergen and Sara knew exactly what that meant.

Mandalay pressed the zipzapexpress button and shouted: "Now everyone - let's swarm like we planned this morning."

Early that morning at the Lincoln Memorial, a message was passed through the crowd mouth to mouth. They didn't use rings for fear the message would be intercepted by the government.

So this is what happened outside the White House: 25,000 kids draped their towels and sleeping bags over the iron fence surrounding the White House so the metal tips were covered. And then all 25,000 kids climbed over the fence and swarmed the White House. President Billingham, his daughters and the government's leaders all saw this unfold via satellite.

"They won't shoot us, they won't touch us and they can't stop us," Mandalay shouted into her ring. The Secret Service issued an emergency alert, hundreds of guards took positions, but they knew with the world watching, they couldn't lay a hand on unarmed, harmless kids.

"Nothing's going to happen dad, they're not going to hurt you," Sara told her father, as the Secret Service rushed into the Oval Office. "They're just gonna sit down in the grass and be cool. But you're gonna have to negotiate with Mandalay Hawk."

Billy was standing outside the Oval Office, in the White House hallway. He pretended to know nothing, but knew everything.

Within 10 minutes, Bergen and Sara whisked Mandalay, Gute, Jazmin and Jonny through the crowd, past security and into the Oval Office.

Chapter 23: "Well, Mr. President, sir..."

P RESIDENT BILLINGHAM'S FIRST THOUGHT WHEN he saw these filthy kids: *For God's sake, give them a bath and what on earth was he doing* **NEGOTIATING WITH THEM!?!**

"It's amazing to meet you," Sara said, as she and Bergen gave Mandalay a big hug.

"Wow, it's amazing to meet you, too. And these are my best buds – Gute and Jazmin."

President Billingham was too shell-shocked to respond. All he could do was stand there in the middle of his famous Oval Office, jaw clenched, shaking his head in despair.

The kids sat on the floor (on the plush, clean carpet!). After hesitating, the president awkwardly twisted himself onto the floor, too. Bottles of water were passed around. Mandalay and her friends drank their first bottles in world record time, then more water was handed out. Under pressure from his daughters, the president ordered the guards to feed and water the kids outside the White House. And Sara told her dad to stop blocking the broadcast, so Jonny took out her Ring-a-Ling-Ding-Ping and began broadcasting live from the Oval Office. This was a good thing, because Jonny's broadcast through *The Sunny Day News* reached far more people than the broadcast through zipzapexpress.

"We don't want any interruptions," Bergen told the Secret Service agent at the door and then shut it in his face. "Now dad, you're going to listen to Mandalay Hawk. She knows what she's talking about. And, as you now know, she's not someone you want to mess with."

As word spread, Jonny's viewership skyrocketed – 500 million people were watching in the U.S. and around the world - and viewers included virtually all of Congress and leaders from countries all over the world.

Tom Hawk, sitting on his couch in front of his dweeb, was awfully proud of his daughter, but shocked that, somehow, she had pulled this off.

Gertrude, of course, was not, as she watched and sipped her tea.

Bushwick was locked in his office mumbling to himself: "*This kid was put on earth to torture me to death.*"

Bushwick's threat of expelling and suspending students remained, but Harkness knew what was important. He invited students to skip test and watch with him. Scores did, jamming into his classroom.

And Judge Baxter, watching in her chambers, said to her clerk, "I knew this girl was destined to do something special, but I didn't expect this."

Mandalay then untied her shoes and took them off. She then removed her socks, which, to be honest, were so disgustingly filthy and sweaty she had to peel them off.

"I'm sorry about my smelly feet, but some things I can't help," she said to the president, who just shook his head.

Mandalay removed the few items on top of the president's desk, placing the phone on the floor and the TOP SECRET papers on a table behind the desk.

"Whoa, what are you doing?" an alarmed President Billingham shouted.

"Mr. President, I need to clear your desk."

"It's ok dad," said Bergen. "We'll put everything back, we promise."

Then Mandalay sat on the desk, feet dangling, and looked directly at the president.

"Well, Mr. President, sir, if I may …"

She was being so polite … because she was about to lecture *The President of the United States in the Oval Office.*

"We go back to before the American Revolution. Farming, hunting and small trade were the dominant ways of life in the colonies and worldwide. There was no mass production, no factories, no electricity, no air pollution ... There was no man-made climate change."

Jazmin jumped up holding a printed diagram she had carried in her backpack.

4.5 billion
years ago....................300,000 years ago......................1784.............................2031
Earth Established   First Homo Sapiens   Industrial Revolution   *Way Too Hot!*

"This simple timeline illustrates what's happened," Mandalay explained, pointing to the paper. "Earth's been around for four and a half billion years, Mr. President. That's *billion* – with a *B*. The modern human species has been around for only a small fraction of that time – approximately 300,000 years. And in just a tiny fraction of those 300,000 years – in about 250 years, with the start of the Industrial Revolution – mankind has managed to start destroying the planet we live on.

"The Industrial Revolution began in 1784, the year James Watt completed his invention of the steam engine. This led to technological advances and eventually to the start of the modern age. The creation of factories and mass production, factories spewing smoke – *pollution* – into the air. The need for more and more power. The need for coal and oil to power things."

Then Gute stood up and took over: "It's hard to digest, hard to understand, Mr. President, but in a very brief period of time, humans have managed to start a catastrophic downward slide. As you can see, for the year 2031, we just wrote three words to sum it up: **WAY TOO HOT!**

"The burning of more and more fossil fuel – fossil fuels are coal, oil and natural gas, because they are really fossils found in the ground - are the main sources of energy to power our modern civilization. The primary source of power for electricity is fossil fuel. Cars, trucks, buses, boats, trains and airplanes burn fossil fuel. Our world has become global, modern, overly extravagant and overly materialistic by burning fossil fuel. More and more factories producing more and more things. Refrigeration. Air conditioning. Processed food. The growing and constant consumer world. Technological advances. First telephones and radios, then TVs, then computers and cell phones, now mindmachines, dweebs and rings. The mass production of everything, the mass transport of everything - *everything* sold and used around the world, including food. People driving, flying, travelling, throughout the world. All this means the burning of more and more fossil fuel."

They were lecturing the president of the United States, who had no choice but to listen.

And the world was watching, via Jonny's broadcast.

Jazmin took over: "When we burn fossil fuels - coal, oil and natural gas - carbon dioxide (aka CO_2) and other dangerous greenhouse gases are produced and released into the air. Carbon dioxide is the primary human-caused, greenhouse gas, Mr. President. The greenhouse gases waft into the air, into the atmosphere and help trap warmth generated by the sun on earth's surface, before it escapes from the atmosphere. This has a devastating cause and effect, Mr. President: The more fossil fuel burned, the more greenhouse gases released into the atmosphere, thus the more heat that is trapped in our atmosphere, making earth hotter and hotter. The process works basically like a glass greenhouse for plants, which allows warming sunlight to enter and heat things up, but then the heat gets trapped and can't escape. The greenhouse gases overheat the air and overheat the world's oceans."

Jazmin took a big swig of water.

The thousands of teens outside the White House, watching on their rings, and the millions watching around the globe, were getting a science lesson, live from the Oval Office.

Then Gute held up his hand-drawn graph.

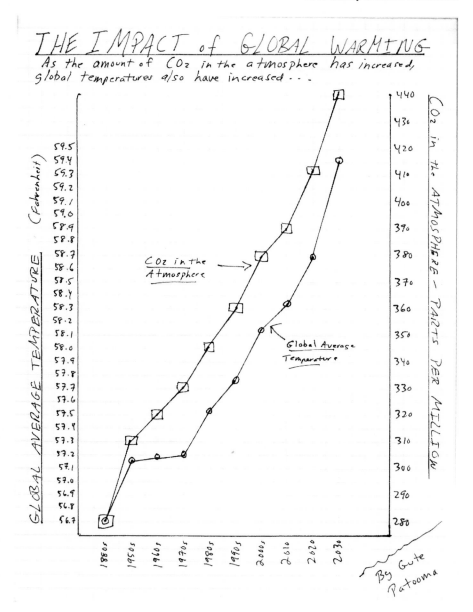

THE IMPACT of GLOBAL WARMING

As the amount of CO_2 in the atmosphere has increased, global temperatures also have increased...

CO_2 in the Atmosphere

Global Average Temperature

CO_2 in the ATMOSPHERE ~ PARTS PER MILLION

GLOBAL AVERAGE TEMPERATURE (Fahrenheit)

By Gute Patooma

Mandalay resumed: "This chart shows the numbers that tell the CO_2 story." She pointed to Gute's graph.

"Mr. President, throughout history," she explained, "for tens of thousands of years, until the start of the Industrial Revolution – the amount of carbon dioxide in the atmosphere was approximately 280 parts per million. Then the amount of CO_2

in the atmosphere began increasing as the world became more developed – more industrialized."

Mandalay pointed to the graph, bottom left. "This chart begins in the year 1880 and then jumps to 1950, after World War II. That's when the world really became more modern and more industrial and the drastic increase in CO_2 in the atmosphere really took off. By the 1950s, the world hit the 300 parts per million number. This means that for every million molecules in the atmosphere, about 300 of those molecules were carbon dioxide. It doesn't seem like a lot, but carbon dioxide molecules have a big impact.

"All this talk about parts per million and molecules is the science gobbledygook that puts everyone to sleep, because it's complicated and because we can't see or taste this CO_2. It's just an abstract number to us. From the 1960s through the 1980s, the CO_2 in the atmosphere continued to increase. By the year 1990, it passed 350 parts per million and was increasing at an alarming rate. Environmentalists were warning that this was a dangerous sign, causing our planet and oceans to warm too much. By 2015, it had passed 400 parts per million ... and it's been going up since. Today, Mr. President, in the year 2031, the CO_2 in the atmosphere has gone past 440 parts per million. A very, very dangerous level."

Mandalay wiped her forehead with her stink towel.

"Remember, Mr. President, the more CO_2 and other greenhouse gases in the atmosphere, the more heat that gets trapped, warming our planet. That's why it's so freakin' hot, that's why we have *The Big Heat* and that's the biggest reason the world is having all these climate-related problems."

Mandalay took a big swig of water. Then she pointed to the graph.

"As you can see here, the average temperatures around the globe have been increasing steadily, almost 3 degrees Fahrenheit hotter in 2030, on average, than it was 150 years ago. This includes the Arctic, Alaska, all the cold parts of the world. And that was before *The Big Heat* came. That was before it became so freakin' hot and we had dumberbummersummer. The average temperature has now increased much, much more than 3 degrees Fahrenheit in many parts of the U.S. and in many parts of the world. Mr. President, these temperature increases, here and elsewhere, are a huge deal. No one predicted such drastic heat so quickly – *no one* - but it happened, Mr. President. Winter is now like August and August is now like a blast furnace. And the U.S., the world leader in most things, is more to blame than any other country."

Mandalay wanted these last words to sink in. She repeated them: "Yes, that's right, Mr. President - *the U.S.* **is** *to blame more than any other country*." She took a long sip of water. She wiped sweat from her brow again. She arched her feet and heard her muscles and bones crack.

Bushwick was watching. He could not believe what he was seeing. *This girl - this delinquent - was lecturing the president of the United States. In the Oval office. Her filthy feet dangling over the side of the famous presidential desk. Like she owned the place.*

Well, in fact, at this moment in time, this nanosecond in world history, Mandalay Hawk and her friends did, kinda, own the place.

Word was spreading fast about the face-to-face in the Oval Office. Viewership had skyrocketed. Three billion people were now watching Jonny's broadcast worldwide. Factories and offices stopped work, traffic froze. Hundreds of millions of kids had told their teachers to get lost, because they wanted to watch Mandalay Hawk and her pals make history.

When the president gave his daughters a dirty look, they smiled and said, "Just chill dad, because you have no choice."

Then Mandalay stood up and looked at the president.

"So, Mr. President, sir, it's fair to say … Yes, Mr. President, sir, it's very fair and accurate to say that we now live in The United States of Anthropocene."

The president's eyebrows shot up. He looked at his daughters, puzzled.

Mandalay nodded at Gute and Jazmin.

Mandalay knew she would need to explain to the president what Anthropocene meant.

"For our viewers out there" – Mandalay stared into Jonny's camera – "Anthropocene is a term used to describe the current scientific – or geological – period in time, a period in time in which humans have impacted earth and climate in a negative way. Anthropos is the Greek word for human being. Yes, this is our period – the human beings period in time – and we are in the process of impacting and destroying the planet we live on. As we know, it began with the Industrial Revolution in the late 1700s, when human activity began to really impact the environment and global climate in a negative way. Another time period, millions of years ago, is one many of you have heard of: The Jurassic period, when dinosaurs roamed the earth.

"Dinosaurs are extinct. Are we next?"

Mandalay stared at the president, let that question linger. Then she stood up.

"So Mr. President," Mandalay continued, "I think it's time we turned off all the lights and the air conditioning."

A disbelieving president looked at his daughters. "It's about a thousand degrees outside!" he shouted, and then realized that was probably the wrong thing to say.

Bergen got up, opened the door to the Oval Office and shouted to the Secret Service agent: "Turn off all the power, now!"

Within a minute, the power was off and the windows were opened.

Mandalay then reached into her backpack. She had planned for this moment, not knowing if it ever would occur.

She pulled out a round candle and placed it on the president's desk and lit it with matches she had brought along.

"Welcome to the new world, Mr. President, a world of radical conservation and radical change," Mandalay said.

He was shaking his head, thinking (again): *Is this kid really, really crazy or what?*

Mandalay smiled. "No, I'm not crazy," she said.

Jeez, she's crazy and she can read my mind, too, he thought, trying to control the thoughts running through his brain.

Tom Hawk was watching, wondering if his daughter had gone too far.

Bushwick was thinking, hopefully, she had.

Gertrude was still watching and knew Mandalay had not.

Mandalay reached into her pocket, pulled out her ring and tossed it high in the air. Jonny was broadcasting this whole thing live – it was a surreal moment. Her camera followed the airborne ring, spinning, twisting, flipping in the Oval Office air, landing in Gute's outstretched hand.

This, like their speeches, had been planned. Yes, Mandalay, Gute and Jazmin do plan, just not the way their parents would have liked.

Gute was holding the ring and not even cringing. He walked over to the desk and from about five feet in the air, dropped it into the garbage can. Jonny, crouching, broadcast this scene to the world.

"Gotta get rid of these things, Mr. President," Gute said. "We have to go back in time – to the use of less and different energy."

President Billingham, and frankly, virtually everyone else, was wondering: *What in God's name are these kids going to do next?*

Gute and Jazmin were now standing on either side of the desk. Gute began making a rhythmic sound with his mouth– *puh-puh, puh-puh, puh-puh.* Then Jazmin began tapping the desk with her hands in sync with Gute – *puh-puh/tap-tap, puh-puh/tap-tap, puh-puh/tap-tap.* They were a human band of two, without instruments.

Then Mandalay jumped up on the president's desk and began dancing slowly to the beat, moving her arms and legs, sliding her bare, dirty feet across the desk.

President Billingham couldn't believe what he was watching. First, it was a lecture atop the desk, now this know-it-all kid who deserved to be locked up was doing some ridiculous doo-hop thingy. She started rapping to the rhythm:

"Yo, yo, yo Mr. President, William "Bucky" Billingham, be a man with a plan ...

Our Democracy made you electable, the people made you selectable.

Don't let us become perishable – avoid being the Prez who's a Fool,

Make sure we're sustainable – so you're remembered as the Prez who's Cool."

Mandalay was bending and twisting with each phrase ...

"Sustainable, sustainable, what a beautiful thought, make sure Mr. President, you can't be bought.

Global warming, the scourge of our earth, renewable energy, the gem of our rebirth.

Swimming in the Hudson in winter, what a freakin' blast, but the reality, this great warming stunner, is really a big fat bummer.

99 degrees in the shade, we no longer have it made.

Glaciers melt and fall, oceans warm and rise, coastal cities drown and crumble under, people tumble all asunder.

Insects populate, diseases propagate.

Droughts desecrate, starvation escalates.

The masses migrate, epidemics depopulate.

Civil unrest spreads and so does hate, then civil wars come and devastate.

And forests burn, destroy and kill, those knowledgeable yearn, but hesitate.

Eliminate carbon pollution, renewables are the solution.

Solar, wind and water, if we don't make that call and convert it all, we'll find that we all fall ... fall ... fall ...

We face the probability, we really do, of having the grand distinction, of dooming our human race to eventual extinction.

Do you want that – Mr. President?"

If ever the world - yes, *the world* ... because something like five billion people were now watching – was stunned silent, this was it.

The rulers of China, Russia, England and France had all cancelled meetings to watch. The Pope had cancelled a prayer session and asked people worldwide to tune in. Even the VP of the United States of Anthropocene had shut her trap and seemed to be tapping her foot.

The Bushwicks were so shocked by what they saw they were unable to move or think. They sat frozen at their desks and watched.

Mr. Harkness had high-fived so many students his arms and hands hurt.

Mandalay Hawk was still standing on the desk, hands on hips, sweating like a sweatbox. She was looking at the president. He was glaring at her.

"You – *you!*" the president shouted angrily, pointing at Mandalay. "You just rapped on the most famous desk in the world." He was too stunned to say anything else. But then, finally, he blurted out, "So - so what do you want me to do?"

Then she started rapping again.

"Well, Mr. President, the man with the plan, bring us your game, you better schmooze and negotiate, heckle, schmeckle and regulate, you better stop global warming now, before people on earth take a big fat bow."

President Billingham held up his hands. "For God's sake, do you think you could just stop that nonsense and tell me what you want me to do?"

Tom Hawk had no idea how his daughter, his clever, very special daughter he loved so much, could have hidden this radical plan from him. Either she is really, really smart, he thought, or this whole thing will backfire and she'll be sent to junior juvie jail for a good long time.

Well, Mandalay wasn't about to let that happen. She was staring at the president.

"You want me to stop rapping, sir. That's fine. Then you better start listening."

Her nice, polite tone was gone.

"This is the 11-point plan," Mandalay demanded. "All across the country, all of these things must be done:

"Number one: By January 1, 2033, all oil, coal and natural gas companies must convert to clean energy production or shut down. If not, they'll have to pay what's called a super duper carbon tax, based on the amount of carbon it releases into the air. And the tax will put them out of business very fast.

"Number two: By January 1, 2033, all factories of all types – whether they make steel or cars or dresses or soap or breakfast cereal or whatever – must convert 100 percent to clean energy use and drastically reduce their overall energy consumption."

Gute's turn, as he stood up: "Number three: The days of gas guzzling cars and trucks are over. By January 1, 2033, all automobiles manufactured in the U.S. and all automobiles driven in the U.S. must be powered by electric battery or solar power. No exceptions.

"Number four: By January 1, 2033, all airplanes manufactured in the U.S. and all airplanes flown in the U.S. must reduce their carbon pollution by 80 percent."

Jazmin's turn, as she stood up: "Number five: By January 1, 2033, all houses, apartments, office buildings and all businesses must convert to clean energy use."

"Number six: By January 1, 2032 – one year earlier - all non-emergency electricity must be shut off between 10:00 p.m. and 6:00 a.m. Countrywide. No exceptions."

The president was shaking his head.

"Don't look at us like we're crazy," Mandalay said. "Adults and politicians screwed it up for so long that it's time for the younger generation to set the rules."

Gute, Jazmin and Mandalay stood next to each other and spoke together: "Number seven: By that same date, January 1, 2032, everyone who lives within 50 miles of work must either walk, bike, swim, boat or take public transportation to work, with one exception. Carpooling (3+ to a car) allowed from 30+ miles from work.

"Number eight: By July 1, 2032, virtually all food: vegetables, fruits, chicken, beef, fish, dairy, baked goods - must be cooked, grown, produced and harvested within a 30-mile radius of where it's sold and eaten. AKA - eat local food!"

"That's all impossible!" an exasperated president exclaimed.

"No, it's not!" all three shot back.

"We have no choice," Mandalay demanded. "If we don't take radical action now - *right now!* - the world will get hotter and all the bad things going on – droughts, floods, forest fires, epidemics, mass migration, starvation, civil wars, etc., etc., – will get worse.

"Number nine," Mandalay continued. "All students at all schools K-12 and at all colleges and universities, effective January 1, 2032, must spend 90 minutes a day studying global warming and its possible solutions. Teachers must be trained, students must be taught. No exceptions."

The president was reduced to just shaking his head.

"Number 10," Mandalay added, "by January 1, 2032, the government must pass strict water rationing laws, including limiting all showers to 90 seconds. New Yorkers do it, so can everyone else."

"Number 11, Mr. President," Mandalay said, "the federal government must start a new cabinet department called the Department of Defeat Human-Caused Global Warming. This department must be in existence within 60 days and it must implement and oversee the plan we just set forth and make additional changes, as needed."

"And Mr. President, we must persuade other countries worldwide to follow our lead and do all these things also," she added, looking right at the president.

President Billingham shook his head again, then raised his arm and pointed a finger at Mandalay.

"You are a punk. You don't know what you're talking about. What you described is *totally impossible, it's preposterous!*" the president shouted angrily.

"No, it's not!" Mandalay, Gute and Jazmin shouted back together, meeting anger with anger.

Mandalay stepped forward and, calmly, said softly, "Mr. President: Do we want the distinction of extinction? Do we, sir?"

Mandalay let that question linger like a dark cloud overhead about to unleash a monsoon on the White House.

And then one kid, just one, a teen from somewhere U.S.A., outside sitting on the White House lawn, said the word "No." He didn't say it particularly loudly, but he said it loud enough that a bunch of kids next to him heard it.

"*No*," he said a second time, a little louder. When he stood up and said **"*No!*"** a third time, louder, kids around him started standing and joined in.

NO!

NO!

Then more kids joined in.

NO!!

NO!!!

NO!!!! to the distinction of extinction.

The president and everyone else in the White House could hear the chant.

No!!!!!!

No!!!!!!

No!!!!!!

And then kids of all ages, in other parts of the U.S., in small towns and big cities, from Bangor, Maine, to Belle Glade, Florida, from Texarkana, Texas, to Kansas City, Kansas, began chanting.

No!!!!!!!!!
No!!!!!!!!!
No!!!!!!!!! to the distinction of extinction.

And then kids in other parts of the world – hundreds of millions now watching on the net - began chanting. In London, Paris, Rome, Amsterdam, Madrid, Istanbul; New Delhi, Nairobi, Moscow, Beijing; Bangkok, Tokyo, Cape Town, Cairo, Jerusalem and on and on. Not sure if the sound could be heard across oceans, but it was shaking continents, stirring souls. There was silence in the Oval Office except for that deafening chant.

No!!!!!!!!!!
No!!!!!!!!!!
No!!!!!!!!!! to the distinction of extinction.

The president just stood there and listened ... a man defeated, dejected, captive in his own sacred office, a captive to a movement that beat all the odds and showed that kids can challenge and defeat all those sucky adults who screwed up.

KRAAP. *Kids Revolt Against Adult Power. It works.* There now was living proof.

The president's daughters were beaming. (And so was Gertrude Johnson, sitting on the edge of her couch, eating popcorn, watching the whole shebang.)

Mandalay looked at Jonny's camera, and held up her hands: "Quiet please, because there's more." And as quickly as the chant of *no* had started, it stopped.

"Here's what's going to happen, Mr. President, worldwide," Mandalay explained. "We shut down coal, oil and natural gas and replace them with clean, renewable energy."

Mandalay held up a piece of paper with a list. "This must happen worldwide," she said. "*Worldwide!*"

Mandalay, Gute and Jazmin stood shoulder to shoulder and spoke together:

"These projects will generate power throughout the world. They'll replace the use of and dependence on fossil fuels. These projects must be coordinated across the globe - because this is a worldwide building effort." They proceeded to read a list of how many wind farms and wind turbines; water turbines, hydro-power plants and dams; solar power plants and rooftop solar panel systems; and other devices and facilities that needed to be built around the world. It totalled in the billions, when you included all the solar panel systems.

"Mr. President," Mandalay said, "all these construction projects must be completed no later than January 1, 2034, but preferably by January 1, 2033. No exceptions, no fooling around ... there's no time to waste."

President Billingham was shaking his head. "You three kids are crazy."

Mandalay ignored that comment. "And Mr. President, in case these numbers can't be reached worldwide fast enough, and the world needs more power short-term to function safely, governments worldwide also must implement super duper carbon-tax programs. This will allow some polluters - coal, gas and oil companies - to continue operation for a very limited time - *but only briefly.*"

"Ludicrous, ridiculous - these kids are out of their minds," an exasperated President Billingham said to his daughters.

"No, Mr. President, we're not out of our minds," Mandalay said. "And we did not make up this plan. We're just three kids with a message. The list of renewable energy sources comes from a very smart and resourceful man, Professor Efram Zumwalt. The other ideas come from a bunch of very smart scientists who study this stuff all day long. It's all they do."

The president rolled his eyes, shook his head and looked at Mandalay like she was a mutant from another planet.

"That's totally, totally, *totally* impossible!" the president continued angrily, turning red. *"Totally! Impossible!"* The president's face and shirt were dripping with sweat.

"Well, Mr. President, it's possible, and it must be done. *Now,*" Mandalay said, calmly.

The president took a breath and then smiled and turned to his daughters.

"Girls, I love you very much, but, unfortunately, your new friends do not know what they're talking about. I understand it's a little hot and probably will get hotter, but their plan is like ... uhm, like, well, flying to Mars tomorrow - *on the back of a giraffe!* Ridiculous, one hundred percent - *no - one thousand percent!* Totally, totally, **totally** *ridiculous! Impossible!"*

Mandalay shook her head. "No, Mr. President, there is no such thing as *impossible*. Everything is possible. And we have American history to prove it."

President Billingham took another deep breath. He then shook his head. He had the unhappy look of a man who had just gone 20 rounds in the boxing ring with a wild and crazy teenager, a teenager who would not give up, would not take no for an answer.

"World War II," Mandalay said.

"What are you talking about?" the president asked.

"World War II is our history lesson."

The president shook his head. "What? Yeah, we defeated the Nazis and Japan and saved the free world. Everyone knows that, young lady."

"Yeah, but it's how we did that, Mr. President. How we won the war is the perfect historical example of how we will defeat global warming today."

Except for the bare and stinky feet, Mandalay was not playing the part of a 14-year-old kid in the Oval Office. She sounded more like a wise college professor lecturing a flunking student.

"World War II was the biggest international emergency the U.S. Government ever faced – *before global warming.* It was worse than 9/11, even worse than the pandemic. And the government took extreme, very, very, *very* extreme action, very, very, *very* quickly.

"In 1939, the U.S. had the 18th largest army in the World, Mr. President, and the U.S. military had manufactured just 2,000 planes that year. But then the Nazis started World War II and the Japanese bombed Pearl Harbor. They were moving to take over much of the free world.

"Do you know what the U.S. did?" Mandalay asked rhetorically, staring at the president.

"The United States of America got serious and went to work. A small army became a huge, 12-million soldier army. The U.S. began building planes at an incredibly quick pace: almost 100,000 planes a year eventually.

"The entire auto industry stopped making cars and began building planes ... and ships and tanks and guns - *everything the army needed.* The average person sacrificed. The U.S. government rationed food, such as butter, milk, eggs, meat, vegetables and fruit. Families started growing their own fruit and vegetables in victory gardens. Within a few years, there were 20 million victory gardens in the U.S - *20 million.* The U.S. government rationed shoes, fabric, oil, cars and lots more. Top business executives from all over the United States left their jobs and agreed to work for the government for $1 a year. That's right: *$1 a year. Everyone sacrificed.*

"The results, Mr. President, show what happens when America puts its mind to something. Today, Mr. President, global warming is our World War III. It's worse than an enemy with guns. It's all around us, impacting everyone and everything we do, and it will only get much worse unless it's defeated.

"It's the 2031 version of the bombing of Pearl Harbor or 9/11, but instead of one location being attacked, the entire world is being bombarded, silently, but deadly, every second of every day. We must do everything we have suggested – and do it now."

"The rest of the world will not listen to us," President Billingham said.

"They'll have no choice," Mandalay explained. "The United States will cut off all relations with any country that does not follow our plan. It's that simple."

"You're a kid just throwing out nonsense. You have no idea what you're talking about."

"I understand exactly what I'm talking about. The U.S. is the most powerful country in the world, the leader of ideas, change, creativity, and business, not to mention good old American consumerism. If countries in Asia, Africa, Europe, South America, etc., want to see the future, they'll follow along with us.

"Mr. President, the world's current lifestyle is unsustainable. We must make radical changes. We have laid out the plan we must take. The plan is not really that complicated. It just needs to be done – *now*."

Mandalay took a long, deep breath. She nodded at Gute and Jazmin. She didn't need to say anymore. She had made her point. She and her friends had made their speeches of a lifetime. Somehow, through hard work, amazing friendship, a miraculous alignment of the stars … and some help from older kids and Gertrude Johnson, the pieces came together, and there they were – speaking to the world, from the Oval Office.

The Bushwicks, still unable to believe what had just happened, were too stunned to even call each other.

Tom Hawk was so, so proud of his daughter. But never – *never in a billion years* – could he have imagined this.

No one could. Not before, not now.

Perhaps the only ones who thought such a thing could happen were Mr. Harkness, who was exhausted from all the high-fiving, and, of course, Gertrude, who told her grandson Billy to get to work on this because she saw Mandalay as a bright and shining light.

Mandalay looked at her friends and winked, a knowing, confident wink. She looked at the president's daughters and nodded, a confident, thank-you kind of nod.

The Sunny Day News was still broadcasting this scene, which by now, by far, was the most watched broadcast or streaming event of all time.

Then Mandalay stepped forward. "Now, Mr. President, we're going to ask you to sign an executive order making all of our demands the law. You've bypassed Congress before. We want you to do it again - now."

"Dad, we love you very much, but none of us," Sara said, motioning to Mandalay and her friends and Jonny – "and none of the thousands of kids outside your window are going anywhere unless you sign this."

Mandalay was holding a printed memo of everything Mandalay, Gute and Jazmin had laid out, from the nighttime blackout period to the new commuting rules, to all the construction projects required to convert to solar, wind and water power.

Mandalay read the document: "I, William "Bucky" Billingham, the President of the United States of America, do hereby agree on behalf of the United States Government and its people, to comply 100 percent with all of the following demands. I agree to these demands and do hereby bind the U.S. government and the American people by signing this executive order."

Mandalay read the list of demands.

Bergen handed her dad a pen and Mandalay handed the document to the president.

The poor president was a sweaty, disheveled, wilted mess.

"Dad, it will be ok," Sara said. "Just sign, save the world, and everyone will go home."

President Billingham thought of his vice president and cabinet - and of everything just thrown in his face. He looked at his daughters, then at Mandalay and her friends. Sweat dripped down his forehead and cheeks.

"I think the proposal is ridiculous. It won't - *can't succeed*. I'm not signing a thing."

He crossed his arms. Jonny's camera was pointing right at him, the world was watching.

"I don't care what anyone thinks. I refuse to sign that document."

This was a moment of silence heard 'round the world. The billions watching held their breath.

"Why not, Mr. President?" Mandalay said in a commanding voice, as she stepped forward.

"Because this is not just a government project. This is a worldwide people project. Everyone has to pitch in, otherwise it will fail."

Mandalay listened and took that in. She looked at her friends. She nodded and then they huddled for a few minutes. Then Mandalay said: "We agree, Mr. President. We left something out."

She grabbed a pen and placed the paper on the president's sacred desk and then wrote on the bottom of the page. Then she looked up.

"I just added the following words to our document, Mr. President," Mandalay said.

"All Americans agree to help defeat global warming by complying with all government requirements, including using much less energy and changing to solar, wind and water power ASAP, and by establishing a Victory Garden - indoors or outdoors, by 2032. Everyone must pitch in. NO EXCEPTIONS. And the U.S. government will work with countries and their people worldwide to make sure this mission is accomplished around the globe."

Mandalay handed the document to the president. "Now, please sign, sir," she said.

The president looked at his daughters as he slowly shook his head. He wiped sweat from his brow. He took a deep breath. Then even a deeper one. He just stood there.

"Ok," he finally said. He took the document, placed it on his desk and signed.

The world saw this via Jonny's ring camera.

It was like a sudden superstorm. Total bedlam erupted on the White House lawn. Thousands and thousands of kids jumped and screamed with joy and threw water bottles and banana skins into the air. It might have registered a 2.5 on the Richter scale.

But Mandalay interrupted the celebration by speaking into Jonny's camera. "This is great, this is fantastic, but we're just starting now," she said, as the world watched on their rings, dweebs, mindmachines or whatever. "The president has signed the document, but now all the work is ahead of us to reduce CO_2 levels and convert to solar, wind and water - ASAP."

The National Guard was called in to truck all the kids home.

Within days, the presidents of the largest companies in the U.S. began resigning and agreed to work for the U.S. government for $1 a year. The largest factories in the U.S. and the world – factories that built cars and planes and rings, dweebs and mindmachines and everything else the consumer-crazy world devoured - began talks to convert to solar, wind and power. And the oil, gas and coal power companies realized their days, finally, were numbered. They understood they had two options: Become a renewable power company, or go out of business.

The headline in many papers worldwide:

Adults Messed it up; Kids Save the World!

Mandalay shook her head and laughed at that headline.

"I don't think so. Our work is just starting," she said to the first reporter who asked.

Bushwick was forced to rescind his expulsions and suspensions. Judge Baxter ripped up her court order and wrote Mandalay a letter, saying "Thank God I gave you a second chance, so you could make history."

A few days later, Mandalay, Gute and Jazmin - and their two dads and one mom - walked the few blocks east to Central Park, on another blistering 105-degree day. Dirt was trucked in, cactus trees were removed and they joined thousands of other New York-ers digging and planting a huge Victory Garden where vegetables would grow. Engineers were already laying pipes to bring in water from the canals to water the garden.

At parks and in backyards all across America, the same thing happened. The goal was to grow vegetables and fruit to feed tens of millions of people. Doing the things needed to stop global warming now became everyone's mission.

Meanwhile, firefighters in 31 states, including California, Oregon, Washington state, Colorado, Texas, the Dakotas, Pennsylvania, New Jersey, Massachusetts, Vermont, Maine and all across New York, struggled to put out forest fires, now called *forever fires*, because they just wouldn't go out. It was so smoggy from the haze from the fires that New Yorkers would not see the sun or the moon clearly for weeks. And because of the smog, everyone had to wear masks again, just like during the pandemic.

"This is a pandemic of heat and drought, and fire and smog that won't end, unless the world changes," Mandalay told PBS during an interview.

That evening, after digging and planting all day, Mandalay, Gute and Jazmin and their parents all decided to go back to the Hawk's apartment for dinner. As it got dark, instead of turning on the lights, Tom Hawk lit a few candles.

And for dinner they ate tomatoes, peppers, cucumbers and lettuce grown on a Brooklyn rooftop garden; cheese made in a Queens' dairy farm; and fresh rice bread from a Harlem bakery. They took off their masks only to eat.

It was a welcome and delicious meal for the new age.

A few days later, Mandalay got a surprise phone call from Gertrude Johnson. Mandalay thanked her for helping get her into the Oval Office. "That was probably the coolest thing I'll ever do," she said to Getrude. Gertrude congratulated Mandalay – and then gave her some startling news. After a lot of pressure from Bergen and Sara, President Billingham had named Gertrude the U.S. government's first Secretary of Defeat Human-Caused Global Warming.

It didn't matter that Gertrude was going on 94 and lived in New York City.

"I don't care how old you are, and you can live in the White House for all I care, as long as you agree to take this job," the president told her.

"Wow, that's amazing," Mandalay said.

Gertrude told Mandalay that she, Gute and Jazmin could work with her if they wanted.

She thanked Gertrude for the offer, but in the end, she, Gute and Jazmin turned her down.

They had school to finish, and they were already thinking about all the work that lay ahead.

Acknowledgements

Writing a book for six years obviously impacted the people around me. I could not have completed this project without the help and support of my wonderful and understanding family: my wife, Emily Russo, and my two daughters, Mabel and Maisy. Emily read many drafts and gave me countless helpful comments along the way.

Mabel always supports me in my writing. She helped me prepare my bibliography as the years dragged on and my work continued. She said she wanted to hold out and read the book after it was published. I can't wait for her to dig in and to see her reaction.

Thanks to Carla Jablonski, a New York City-based editor, for reading an early draft of my manuscript and making excellent suggestions. She's an editor with a good sense of story.

Thanks to Professor Richard B. Primack, author of *Walden Warming: Climate Change Comes to Thoreau's Woods,* and a professor of biology at Boston University, for spending time with Mabel and me at Walden's Pond one spring day and educating us about how climate change had impacted the pond and the world Henry David Thoreau studied and wrote about in the 1850s. Professor Primack reviewed a draft of my book and made helpful comments, for which I am grateful.

I also would like to thank Mark Cane, the G. Unger Vetlesen Professor Emeritus of Earth and Climate Sciences at Columbia University, for reviewing a draft of my manuscript and making helpful comments.

I also would like to thank Mark Z. Jacobson, a professor of civil and environmental engineering at Stanford University, for reviewing a portion of my manuscript.

Thank you to the good people at Bowne Printers on Water Street, in New York City, for their excellent tutorial on the use of a printing press.

I also would like to recognize the thousands of scientists and journalists around the world who have been studying and writing about climate change for decades and who have brought these urgent issues to the world's attention.

Many scientists and journalists have distinguished themselves in this field, including Elizabeth Kolbert, James Hansen and Bill McKibben.

And thank you to my good and old friends Alec Cecil and Michael Simon for reviewing an early draft and making helpful editorial comments.

Selective Bibliography

(Although this book is a work of fiction set in 2030-31, with made up characters and some science fiction projected into the future, the fiction is mixed with a lot of real science. Below are most of the books, articles and reports I read as research for this book.)

Abrams, Lindsay. "Global Warming is Going to Hammer New York: New Study Reveals a Future of Downpours, Rising Seas." *Salon.com*, February 17, 2015.

Alter, Charlotte; Haynes, Suyin; and Worland, Justin. "The Conscience." *Time*, Person of the Year Issue (Greta Thunberg), December 23-30, 2019.

American Association for the Advancement of Science. *What We Know: The Reality, Risks, and Response to Climate Change*, 2014.

Ameshistory.org/exhibits/events/rationing. *World War 11 Rationing on the U.S. Homefront*, January 20, 2015.

Anderson, Kevin. "Climate change going beyond dangerous - Brutal numbers and tenuous hope." *Climate Development and Equity: Development Dialogue*, September 2012.

Appunn, Kerstine. "Germany's Greenhouse Gas Emissions and Climate Targets." *Clean Energy Wire*, February 19, 2015.

The Associated Press (via The Berkshire Eagle). *UN: Climate Change Means More Weather Disasters Every Year*, Oct. 13, 2020.

Atcheson, John. "The Paris Climate Conference: Playing Craps with Our Planet's Future." *CommonDreams.org*, September 1, 2016.

Baron, Laignee. "143 Million People Could Soon Be Displaced Because of Climate Change, World Bank Says." *Time* (via Time.com), March 20, 2018.

Bloomberg, Michael R. "Realistic Goals for the Paris Climate Conference." *The Wall Street Journal*, June 28, 2015.

Blue Green Alliance. *Climate Works for All: A Platform for Reducing Emissions, Protecting Our Communities, and Creating Good Jobs for New Yorkers,* December 18, 2014.

Bonneuil, Christophe and Fressoz, Jean-Baptiste. *The Shock of the Anthropocene.* London and New York: Verso, 2017.

Borth, Christy. *Masters of Mass Production.* Indianapolis and New York: The Bobbs-Merrill Company, 1945.

Branigan, Tania. "Joshua Wong: The Teenager Who is the Public Face of the Hong Kong Protests." *The Guardian,* October 1, 2014.

Brannen, Peter. *The Ends of the World: Volcanic Apocalypses, Lethal Oceans, and Our Quest to Understand Earth's Past Mass Extinctions.* New York. Ecco (HarperCollins Publishers), 2017.

Brune, Michael. "From Walden to the White House." *Huffingtonpost.com,* January 22, 2013.

Buckley, Cara. "Is there a Cure for My Climate Grief?" *The New York Times,* November 17, 2019.

Buckley, Chris, and Wong, Alan. "At 17, Setting Off Protests That Roil Hong Kong." *The New York Times,* October 1, 2014.

Buckley, Chris. "China Burns Much More Coal Than Reported, Complicating Climate Talks." *The New York Times,* November 3, 2015.

Britannica Online Encyclopedia. "James Watt." *Britannica.com,* January 9, 2018.

Buzan, Jonathan; Huber, Matthew; and Robert Kopp. "The Deadly Combination of Heat and Humidity." *The New York Times,* June 7, 2015.

Cabbage, Michael and McCarthy, Leslie. "NASA Science Leads New York City Climate Change 2015 Report." *NASA.gov,* February 18, 2015.

Callaway, Ewen. "Oldest Homo Sapiens Fossil Claim Rewrites Our Species' History." *Nature,* June 7, 2017.

Cardwell, Diane. "Copenhagen Lighting the Way to Greener, More Efficient Cities." *The New York Times,* December 8, 2014.

Cardwell, Diane. "Fueled by Danish Ingenuity." *The New York Times,* January 18, 2015.

Cardwell, Diane. "Wind Power Is poised To Spread To All States." *The New York Times,* May 20, 2015.

Cardwell, Diane. "Tackling Climate Change, One Class at a Time." *The New York Times*, July 1, 2015.

Carson, Rachel. *Silent Spring*. New York: Mariner (Houghton Mifflin Harcourt Publishing Company), 1962, 2002.

Casey, Nicholas. "Climate Change Claims a Lake and a Centuries-Old Identity." *The New York Times*, July 8, 2016.

Census.gov, 2013 population estimates.

Center for Constitutional Rights. *Statement of the Plaintiffs' Attorneys in Wiwa v. Royal Dutch/ Shell*, June 8, 2009.

Chambers, Madeline. "Germany Steps Up CO2 Cuts to Meet 2020 Climate Goals." *Thomson Reuters*, December 3, 2014.

Cho, Renee. "Is Biomass Really Renewable?" *State of the Planet*, Earth Institute, Columbia University, August 18, 2011, updated October 19, 2016.

Chow, Lorraine. "100 percent renewable energy worldwide isn't just possible, it's more cost-effective than existing systems." *AlterNet* (via Salon.com), December 23, 2017.

Citizens' Climate Lobby. *citizensclimatelobby.org*, various articles.

Clemens, Danny. "Climate Change by the Numbers: 760 Million Displaced by Rising Sea Levels." *Discovery.com*, January 15, 2018.

Climate Central. "These U.S. Cities Are Most Vulnerable to Major Coastal Flooding and Sea Level Rise." *ClimateCentral.org*, October 25, 2017.

Climate Central. "The Globe is Already Above 1 degree C, on Its Way to 1.5 degrees C." *ClimateCentral.org*, October 9, 2018.

Cohen, Patricia. " 'This is biblical proportion. Nothing like this has ever been seen.' " *The New York Times*, July 31, 2019.

Collins, Glenn. "Using Central Park to Study Global Warming and Flooding." *The New York Times*, September 14, 2005.

Conley, Jessica. "Here's why hurricanes are a rarity in Maine." *New Center Maine* (http://www.newscentermaine.com/article/weather/blogs/heres-why-hurricanes-are-a-rarity-in-maine/97-593136612), Sept. 11, 2018.

Conway, Erik M. and Oreskes, Naomi. *The Collapse of Western Civilization: A View from the Future*. New York: Columbia University Press, 2014.

Coolearth (www.coolearth.org), *IPCC Global Warming Special Report 2018/What does it actually mean?* October 8, 2019.

co2.earth. *Are we stabilizing yet?* October 17, 2019.

co2now.org. Various reports, 2015.

Cullen, Heidi. "What Weather Is the Fault of Climate Change?" *The New York Times*, March 11, 2016.

Cullen, Heidi. "Think It's Hot? Just Wait." *The New York Times*, August 21, 2016.

Dahlman, LuAnn. "Climate Change: Global Temperature." *Climate.gov*. April 19, 2017.

Dahlman, LuAnn. "Climate Change: Global Temperature." *Climate.gov*. September 11, 2017.

Dastagir, Alia E. "Largest - Ever – Climate Change March Rolls Through NYC." *USAToday.com*, September 22, 2014.

Davenport, Coral. "Pentagon Signals Security Risks of Climate Change." *The New York Times*, October 13, 2014.

Davenport, Coral. "With Compromises, a Global Accord to Fight Climate Change Is in Sight." *The New York Times*, December 10, 2014.

Davenport, Coral. "Legal Battle Begins Over Obama Bid to Curb Greenhouse Gases." *The New York Times*, April 16, 2015.

Davenport, Coral. "As Coal Fades, Who Will Keep the Lights On?" *The New York Times*, April 23, 2015.

Davenport, Coral. "White House Gives Conditional Approval for Shell to Drill in Arctic." *The New York Times*, May 11, 2015.

Davenport, Coral. "Nations Approve Landmark Climate Accord in Paris." *The New York Times*, December 12, 2015.

Davenport, Coral and Robertson, Campbell. "Resetting the First American 'Climate Refugees'." *The New York Times*, May 3, 2016.

Davenport, Coral, and Pierre-Louis, Kendra. "U.S. Climate Report Warns of Damaged Environment and Shrinking Economy." *The New York Times*, November 23, 2018.

Davenport, Coral. "Trump Administration's Strategy on Climate: Try to Bury Its Own Scientific Report." *The New York Times*, November 25, 2018.

Davenport, Coral, and Friedman, Lisa. "How Trump is Ensuring That Greenhouse Gas Emissions Will Rise." *The New York Times*, November 26, 2018.

Davis, Julie Hirschfeld; Landler, Mark; and Davenport, Coral. " 'Terrifying' Path of Climate Crisis Weighs on Obama." *The New York Times*, September 8, 2016.

De Aenlle, Conrad. "Renewables' Hope Springs Long-Term." *The New York Times*, April 23, 2015.

Denayer, Will. "How climate change is rapidly taking the planet apart." *Ecology and Growth, www.flassbeck-economics.com*, July 20, 2016.

DePalma, Anthony. "A Mayor's Green-Power Moonshot." *The New York Times*, April 23, 2015.

Diffenbaugh, Noah S. "How We Know it was Climate Change." *The New York Times*, December 31, 2017.

DoSomething.org. *11 Facts about Global Warming.* February 19, 2015.

Energy Informative. "How Can We Use Geothermal Energy?" *Energyinformative. org*, May 3, 2013.

Environmental Defense Fund (www.edf.org), *This is why fighting climate change is so important*, September 20, 2019.

Environmental Protection Agency. *EPA.gov*, 2014 – 20120, various articles.

Environmental Protection Agency. "Fact Sheet: Clean Power Plan by the Numbers," *EPA.gov*, September 24, 2015.

Environmental Protection Agency. "Climate Change Indicators in the United States, 2014." *EPA.gov*.

Environmental Protection Agency. "Climate Change Indicators: Atmospheric Concentrations of Greenhouse Gases." *EPA.gov*, updated April 2016.

Environmental Protection Agency. "Climate Change Impacts: Climate Impacts on Agriculture and Food Supply." *EPA.gov*, January 19, 2017.

Environmental Protection Agency. "Overview of Greenhouse Gases." *EPA.gov*, updated April 11, 2019.

Fitzpatrick, John W. and Senner, Nathan R. "The Globe's Greatest Travelers Are Dying." *The New York Times*, April 29, 2018.

Flannery, Tim. *Atmosphere of Hope: Searching for Solutions to the Climate Crisis.* New York: Atlantic Monthly Press, 2015.

Flavelle, Christopher. "Climate Change Threatens the World's Food Supply, United Nations Warns." *The New York Times*, August 8, 2019.

Friedman, Lisa. *The New York Times*, Climate Fwd: newsletter, October 10, 2018.

Foderaro, Lisa W. "Canvassing Central Park and Finding New Tenants." *The New York Times*, August 27, 2013.

Forbes.com. *The World's Biggest Public Companies List*, 2014.

Fountain, Henry. "Energy Options Ebb and Grow: Nuclear: Carbon Free, But not Free of Unease." *The New York Times*, December 23, 2014.

Fountain, Henry. "It's Like It Never Left: Another El Nino May Be on the Way." *The New York Times*, April 13, 2017.

Fountain, Henry. "What is a 'Bomb Cyclone?' " *The New York Times*, January 3, 2018.

Fountain, Henry. "Why So Cold? Climate Change May Be Part of the Answer." *The New York Times*, January 3, 2018.

Fountain, Henry. "How Hot Was July? Hotter Than Ever, Global Data Shows." *The New York Times*, August 5, 2019.

Fountain, Henry. "CO_2 Levels Are Piling Up 'Like Trash In a Landfill." *The New York Times*, June 4, 2020.

Frank, Adam. "Is Climate Disaster Inevitable?" *The New York Times*, January 18, 2015.

Friedman, Lisa. Climate Fwd: newsletter. *The New York Times*, Oct. 10, 2018.

Funk, McKenzie. "The Wreck of the Kulluk." *The New York Times Magazine*, January 4, 2015.

Gillis, Justin. "U.N. Panel Issues Its Starkest Warning Yet on Global Warming." *The New York Times*, November 2, 2014.

Gillis, Justin. "3.6 Degrees of Uncertainty." *The New York Times*, December 16, 2014.

Gillis, Justin. "2014 Was Hottest Year on Record, Surpassing 2010." *The New York Times*, January 16, 2015.

Gillis, Justin. "Verbal Warning: Labels in the Climate Debate." *The New York Times*, February 17, 2015.

Gillis, Justin and Schwartz, John. "Deeper Ties to Corporate Cash for Doubtful Climate Researcher." *The New York Times*, February 22, 2015.

Gillis, Justin and Somini Sengupta. "Limited Progress Seen Even as More Nations Step Up on Climate." *The New York Times*, September 28, 2015.

Gillis, Justin. "2015 Likely to Be Hottest Year Ever Recorded." *The New York Times*, October 21, 2015.

Gillis, Justin. "Short Answers to Hard Questions About Climate Change." *The New York Times*, November 11, 2015.

Gillis, Justin. "A Path for Climate Change, Beyond Paris." *The New York Times*, December 1, 2015.

Gillis, Justin. "Climate Model Predicts West Antarctic Ice Sheets Could Melt Rapidly." *The New York Times*, March 30, 2016.

Gillis, Justin. "Global Warming's Mark: Coastal Inundation." *The New York Times*, September 4, 2016.

Gillis, Justin and Schwartz, John. "Earth Sets a Temperature Record for the Third Straight Year." *The New York Times*, January 18, 2017.

Global Warming Facts. "Top 50 Things To Do to Stop Global Warming." *Globalwarming-facts.info*, February 19, 2015.

Glusac, Elaine. "Carbon- Free Cooking in Thailand." *The New York Times*, October 1, 2015.

Gollier, Christian and Tirole, Jean. "Making Climate Agreements Work." *The Economist*, June 1, 2015.

Goodstein, Laurie and Yardley, Jim. "Pope Francis, in Sweeping Encyclical, Calls for Swift Action on Climate Change." *The New York Times*, June 18, 2015.

Gorman, James. "Nature in the Balance: The trade-offs of climate change: Bears look to geese, geese look to new lands, and new lands suffer." *The New York Times*, September 23, 2014.

Graw, Michael (Oceanography, Oregon State University). "Only eight hurricanes hit New England in 100 years. Soon more will head for Boston" (https://massivesci..com/articles/climate-change-more-hurricanes-new-york-boston/).

MassiveScience.org, Nov. 6, 2017.

Greenhouse Development Rights Project. *gdrights.org*, 2015.

Greenstone, Michael. "If We Dig Out All Our Fossil Fuels, Here's How Hot We Can Expect It to Get." *The New York Times*, April 8, 2015.

Guangcheng, Chen. "The Barefoot Lawyer: A Blind Man's Fight for Justice and Freedom in China." New York: Henry Holt, 2015.

Hamilton, Clive. "Risks of Climate Change." *The New York Times*, February 12, 2015.

Hansen, James, et al. Interactive Comment on "Ice Melt, sea level rise and super-storms: evidence from paleoclimate data, climate modeling and modern observations that 2 degrees C global warming is highly dangerous." *Atmospheric Chemistry and Physics*, open access, discussions. July 27, 2015; August 4, 2015; and August 20, 2015.

Hansen, James. *Congressional Testimony of Dr. James Hansen, June 23, 1988.* www.sealevel.info.

Hansen, James. *Storms of my Grandchildren*. New York: Bloomsbury, 2009.

Hansen, James. "Environmental and Development Challenges: The Imperative of a Carbon Fee and Dividend." *Oxford Online Handbooks,* May 2015.

Hansen, James. *Darn!! Sea Level Disaster Ahead! In 200-900 Years. When?* July 27, 2015.

Hansen, James and Sato, Makiko. *Predictions Implicit in 'Ice Melt' Paper and Global Implications.* September 21, 2015.

Hansen, James. *Isolation of 1600 Pennsylvania Avenue: Part 1.* November 27, 2015.

Hansen, James. *Winning Workshop + Beijing Charts + Year-End Comments.* December 29, 2015.

Hansen, James; Lo, Ken; Ruedy, Reto; Sato, Makiko; and Schmidt, Gavin A. "Global Temperature in 2015." *Climate Science, Awareness and Solutions*, Earth Institute, Columbia University, January 19, 2016.

Hansen, James. *I am an Energy Voter.* February 23, 2016.

Hansen, James and Sato, Makiko. *Regional Climate Change and National Responsibilities.* March 1, 2016.

Hansen, James. *Our Children's Right to a Viable Future.* March 9, 2016.

Hansen, James. *Ice Melt, Sea Level Rise and Super Storms: The Threat of Irreparable Harm.* March 22, 2016.

Hansen, James. *Dangerous Scientific Reticence.* March 23, 2016.

Hansen James. *Hypocrites Unite: AGU and ExxonMobil.* April 15, 2016.

Hansen, James. *Mr. Buffett's Ark (letter to Warren Buffett).* April 27, 2016.

Hansen, James. *Remarks at Berkshire Hathaway Shareholder Meeting.* April 30, 2016.

Hansen, James. *Canadian Common Sense: Petition #e297.* May 16, 2016.

Hansen, James and Sato, Makiko. *A Better Graph.* September 26, 2016.

Hansen, James. *Young People's Burden.* October 4, 2016.

Hansen, James. *Letter to Prime Minister Solberg of Norway.* The Earth Institute of Columbia University, October 18, 2016.

Hansen, James. *Washington Can Lead: Unwashed Version.* October 26, 2016.

Hansen, James. *Carbon Pricing: A Useful Cautionary Tale.* October 28, 2016.

Hansen, James. *Climate Change Call to Action.* October 31, 2016.

Hansen, James. *Rolling Stones.* January 11, 2017.

Hansen, James. "Thirty years later, what needs to change in our approach to climate change." *Boston Globe*, June 27, 2018.

Harris, Gardiner. "Borrowed Time on Disappearing Land." *The New York Times*, March 28, 2014.

Harris, Gardiner. "Obama Defends Presence at Climate Change While Syria War Rages." *The New York Times*, December 1, 2015.

Hayes, Christopher. "The New Abolitionism." *The Nation*, April 22, 2014.

Hayhoe, Katharine. "The Christian Case for Climate Action." *The New York Times*, November 3, 2019.

Helm, Burt. "The Climate Bottom Line." *The New York Times*, February 1, 2015.

Herbert, Geoff. "Middle Child's Day: Syracuse University Grad Calls for Mid-Kids to go on 'strike' Aug. 12." *Syracuse.com*, July 26, 2013.

Herman, Arthur. *Freedom's Forge: How American Business Produced Victory in World War II.* New York: Random House, Inc., 2012.

Historic Hallowell (http://historichallowell.mainememory.nt/page/1971/display.html). *Hurricanes of 1954 - Stories and Timelines*, Oct. 2, 2020.

Hope, Mat. "Dissecting Germany's New Climate Action Plan." *Carbon Brief*, December 4, 2014.

Hubler, Shawn. "Is This the End of Summer as We've Known It?" *The New York Times*, July 29, 2021.

Huebner, Kalle."2,000 Watt Society." *Ourworld.unu.edu*, June 2, 2009.

Hurricanesciene.org (http://www.hurricanescience.org/history/storms/1990s/bob/). *Hurricanes: Science and Society, 1991 - Hurricane Bob.* Nov. 2, 2020.

Intergovernmental Panel on Climate Change (IPCC), 2018: *Global Warming of 1.5°C. An IPCC Special Report on the impacts of global warming of 1.5°C above pre-industrial levels and related global greenhouse gas emission pathways, in the context of strengthening the global response to the threat of climate change, sustainable development, and efforts to eradicate poverty.* [Masson-Delmotte, V., P. Zhai, H.-O. Pörtner, D. Roberts, J. Skea, P.R. Shukla, A. Pirani, W. Moufouma-Okia, C. Péan, R. Pidcock, S. Connors, J.B.R. Matthews, Y. Chen, X. Zhou, M.I. Gomis, E. Lonnoy, T. Maycock, M. Tignor, and T. Waterfield (eds.)]. In Press. October 8, 2018.

IPCC, 2021: Summary for Policymakers. In: *Climate Change 2021: The Physical Science Basis. Contribution of Working Group I to the Sixth Assessment Report of the Intergovernmental Panel on Climate Change* [Masson- Delmotte, V., P. Zhai, A. Pirani, S. L. Connors, C. Péan, S. Berger, N. Caud, Y. Chen, L. Goldfarb, M. I. Gomis, M. Huang, K. Leitzell, E. Lonnoy, J. B. R. Matthews, T. K. Maycock, T. Waterfield, O. Yelekçi, R. Yu and B. Zhou (eds.)]. Cambridge University Press. In Press. August 8, 2021.

Jacobson, Mark Z. and Mark A. Delucchi. "A Plan for Sustainable Future: How to Get All Energy from Wind, Water and Solar Power by 2026." *Scientific American*, November 2009.

Jacobson, Mark Z. and Mark A. Delucchi. "Providing all Global Energy with Wind, Water and Solar Power, Part 1: Technologies, Energy Resources, Quantities and Areas of Infrastructure, and Materials." *Energy Policy 39* (2011) at Elsevier.com.

Jacobson, Mark Z., et al. "Examining the Feasibility of Converting New York State's All-Purpose Energy Infrastructure to One Using Wind, Water and Sunlight." *Energy Policy 57* (2013) at Elsevier.com.

Jacobson, Mark Z., et al. "100% Clean and Renewable Wind, Water, and Sunlight All-Sector Energy Roadmaps for 139 Countries of the World," *Joule 1*, pages 108-121, September 6, 2017.

Jaggard, Victoria. "Why did the dinosaurs go extinct?" *National Geographic* (www.nationalgeographic.com), July 31, 2019.

Jawort, Adrian. "The Declaration of Independence - Except for 'Indian Savages'." *Indian Country Today Media Network.com*, May 13, 2014.

Jones, Nicola. "How the World Passed a Carbon Threshold and Why it Matters." *e360.yale.edu*, January 26, 2017.

Jordan, Rob. "Stanford Researcher Maps Out an Alternative Energy Future for New York." *Stanford.edu*, March 12, 2013.

Kahn, Brian. "This is the Globe's Hottest Five-Year Period Record." *climatecentral. org*, November 25, 2015.

Kivlehan, Sophie, and James Hansen. *Young People's Burden: Averting Climate Disaster*. Presentation at COP-3 meeting in Bonn, Germany, November 6, 2017.

Klein, Naomi. *This Changes Everything: Capitalism vs. the Climate*." New York: Simon and Schuster, 2014.

Kolbert, Elizabeth. "The Weight of the World: Can Christiana Figueres Persuade Humanity to Save Itself?" *The New Yorker*, August 24, 2015.

Kolbert, Elizabeth. *The Sixth Extinction: An Unnatural History*. New York: Henry Holt and Company, 2014.

Kormann, Carolyn. "New York's Original Teen-Age Climate Striker Welcomes A Global Movement." *The New Yorker*, September 20, 2019.

Kristof, Nicholas. "Temperatures Rise, and We're Cooked." *The New York Times*, September 11, 2016.

Landler, Mark and Perlez, Jane. "U.S. and China Set Aside Rifts for Climate Accord." *The New York Times*, September 4, 2016.

Landler, Mark; Plumer, Brad; and Qiu, Linda. "A Long List of Economic Burdens, Bolstered by Dubious Data." *The New York Times*, June 2, 2017.

Landler, Mark and Coral Davenport. "Climate Warning Hits Silent Wall on Trump's Desk." *The New York Times*, October 9, 2018.

Leahy, Stephen. "Polar Bears Really Are Starving Because of Global Warming, Study Shows." *National Geographic* (reviewed at NationalGeographic.com), February 1, 2018.

Leahy, Stephen. "How to erase 10 years of carbon emissions? Plant trees - lots of them." *National Geographic*, July 4, 2019.

Leber, Rebecca. "This is What Our Hellish World Will Look Like After We Hit the Global Warming Tipping Point." *The New Republic*, December 21, 2014.

Levine, Alexandra S. "New York Today: Return of the Rats." *The New York Times*, August 17, 2016.

Linden, Eugene. "How Scientists Got It So Wrong." *The New York Times*, November 10, 2019.

Lohr, Steve. "Homes Try To Reach Smart Switch." *The New York Times*, April 23, 2015.

Magra, Iliana; Peltier, Elian; and Meheut, Constant. "Record Heat Melts Europe, and Relief Is Scarce." *The New York Times*, July 26, 2019.

Maine Emergency Management Agency

(https://www.maine.gov/mema/hazards/natural-hazards/hurricanes). *Hurricanes*, Oct. 2, 2020.

Mandery, Evan J. "The Missing Campus Climate Debate." *The New York Times*, November 1, 2014.

Markham, Lauren. "Fleeing a Warmer World," *The New York Times*, July 1, 2018.

McKibben, Bill. *The End of Nature*. New York: Random House, Inc., 1989.

McKibben, Bill. *Eaarth: Making a Life on a Tough New Planet*. New York: St. Martin's Press, 2010.

McKibben, Bill (editor). *The Global Warming Reader*. New York: Penguin Books, 2012.

McKibben, Bill. "Global Warming's Terrifying New Math." *Rolling Stone*, July 19, 2012.

McKibben, Bill. "Climate: Will We Lose the Endgame?" *The New York Review of Books*, July 10, 2014.

McKibben, Bill. "The Pope and the Planet." *The New York Review of Books*, August 13, 2015.

McKibbon, Bill. "A Very Grim Forecast." *The New York Review of Books*, November 22, 2018.

McKibbon, Bill. *Falter: Has the Human Game Begun to Play Itself Out?* New York: Henry Holt and Company, 2019.

McKibbon, Bill. "130 Degrees." *The New York Review of Books*, August 20, 2020.

Mulvaney, Kierna. "Climate Change report card: These countries are reaching targets." *National Geographic*, September 19, 2019.

Murphy, Laura W. "Historic Reading of the Declaration of Independence by African American Descendant of Singer." *ACLU.org*, July 2, 2012.

Nagourney, Adam. "California Governor Orders New Target for Emissions Cuts." *The New York Times*, April 29, 2015.

Najar, Nida and Kumar, Hari. "In a Scorched India, Heat Wave Sets a Record." *The New York Times*, May 21, 2016.

NASA. "A Blanket around the Earth." *NASA.gov*, February 19, 2015.

NASA. "NASA, NOAA Data Show 2016 Warmest Year on Record Globally." *NASA. gov*, January 18, 2017.

NASA. "World of Change: Global Temperatures." *NASA.gov*, May 29, 2017.

NASA. "Global Climate Change: Vital Signs of the Planet." *NASA.gov*, various articles, 2014-2018.

NASA. "Carbon Dioxide: Latest Measurement." *NASA.gov*, Aug. 2. 2021.

National Centers for Environmental Information. *Global Summary Information for 2015*. December 2015.

National Centers for Environmental Information. *Global Climate Report – June 2017*. June 2017.

National Geographic. "Cool It. The Climate Issue." November 2015.

National Geographic. "Did You Hear the One About the Neanderthal" (Interview with Ella Al-Shamahi), 2016.

National Snow and Ice Data Center. "State of the Cryosphere: Is the Cryosphere sending signals about Climate Change?" *inside.org/cryosphere*, January 15, 2018.

The National World War II Museum. New Orleans (www.nww2m.com). *Victory Gardens in World War II*, 2015.

The National World War II Museum. New Orleans (www.nww2m.com). *WW II by the Numbers*, 2017.

Natural History Museum. London (nhm.ac.uk). The Dino Directory.

Natural Resources Defense Council. *The Climate Stewardship Act Fact Sheets*, March 18, 2005.

The New York City Panel on Climate Change. Report 2015.

The New York Times, Editorial. "Hydrogen Cars, Coming Down the Pike." November 29, 2014.

The New York Times, Editorial. "More Momentum for the Climate Summit." October 4, 2015.

The New York Times, Editorial. "Climate Change News That Stuck With Us in 2016." December 14, 2016.

The New York Times Magazine, "The Climate Issue," July 26, 2020.

NOAA National Climate Data Center. *State of the Climate: Global Analysis for Annual 2014*, http://www.ncdc.noaa.gov/sotc/global/.

Nordhaus, William D. "A New Solution: The Climate Club." *The New York Review of Books*, June 4, 2015.

Olson, Kay Melchisedech, (Illustrated by Tod Smith). *Johann Gutenberg and the Printing Press*. Capstone Press, 2007.

Oreskes, Naomi and Conway, Erik M. *The Collapse of Western Civilization: A View from the Future*. New York: Columbia University Press, 2014.

Oborn, Liz. "History of Changes in the Earth's Temperature." *CurrentResults.com*, July 1, 2017.

Osnos, Evan. "A Blind Lawyer vs. Blind Chinese Power." *The New York Review of Books*, July 9, 2015.

Owings, Alison. "The Damaging Three Words of the Declaration of Independence." *HuffingtonPost.com*, July 2, 2011.

Owings, Alison. "The Declaration of Independence, Jefferson's 'Merciless Indian Savages,' and getting Flamed on Huffington Post." *Indian Country Today Media Network.com*, July, 7, 2011.

Patel, Jugal K. "Shelf Grew 17 Miles in the Last Two Months." *The New York Times*, February 7, 2017.

Phys.org. Climate change aggravates global hunger: UN, September 15, 2017.

Pierre-Louis, Kendra. "NASA said 2017 was the second-warmest year on record." *The New York Times*, January 18, 2018.

Pierre-Louis, Kendra. "Bigger Avalanches are Being Set Off by Climate Change." *The New York Times*, January 26, 2018.

Pierre-Louis, Kendra. "Climate Change Is Fueling Wildfires Nationwide, New Report Warns." *The New York Times*, November 27, 2018.

Pierre-Louis, Kendra. "Greenhouse Gas Emissions Accelerate Like a 'Speeding Freight Train' in 2018." *The New York Times*, December 6, 2018.

Pierre-Louis, Kendra. "Ocean Temperatures Rising Faster, as Are Fears." *The New York Times*, January 11, 2019.

Pilkington, Ed. "Shell Pays Out 15.5M Over Saro-Wiwa Killing." *The Guardian*, June 8, 2009.

Plumber, Brad, and Fountain, Henry. "A Hotter Future is Certain, Climate Panel Warns. But How Hot is Up To Us." *The New York Times*, Aug. 8, 2021.

Plumer, Brad, and Popovich, Nadja. "The World Still Isn't Meeting Its Climate Goals." *The New York Times*, December 7, 2018.

Plumer, Brad. "U.S. Carbon Emissions Surged in 2018 Even as Coal Plants Closed." *The New York Times*, January 8, 2019.

Popovich, Nadja; Schwarz, John; and Schlossberg, Tatiana. "How Americans Think About Climate Change, in Six Maps." *The New York Times*, March 21, 2017.

Popovich, Nadja. "Jobs Are in Solar, Not Coal." *The New York Times*, April 25, 2017.

Porter, Eduardo. "Invisible Hand Is Kept Off Carbon." *The New York Times*, June 1, 2015.

Porter, Eduardo. "Climate Deal Badly Needs a Big Stick." *The New York Times*, June 2, 2015.

Porter, Eduardo. "Climate Change Calls For Science, Not Hope." *The New York Times*, June 23, 2015.

Presidency.ucsb.edu. *The American Presidency Project: Franklin D. Roosevelt, Statement Encouraging Victory Gardens.* February 10, 2015.

Primack, Richard B. *Walden Warming: Climate Change Comes to Thoreau's Woods.* Chicago: University of Chicago Press, 2014.

Princeton Environmental Institute. Princeton University, Carbon Mitigation Initiative. Various reports and articles, 2011-2015.

Quinnipiac University, National (US) Poll (on climate change), August 29, 2019.

Radford, Tim. "Warming raised threat of global famine repeat." Climate News Network (https://climatenewsnetwork.net/), October 19, 2018.

remembersarowiwa.com. Various articles.

Rhodium Group report. *Preliminary US Emissions Estimates for 2018.* January 8, 2019.

Rich, Nathaniel. "Losing Earth: The decade we almost stopped climate change. A tragedy in two acts." *The New York Times Magazine*, August 5, 2018.

Ripple, William J.; Wolf, Christopher: Newsome, Thomas M.; Galetti, Mauro; Alamgir, Mohammed; Crist, Eileen; Mahmoud, Mahmoud I.; Laurance, William F.; and 15,364 scientist signatories from 184 countries. "World Scientists' Warning to Humanity: A Second Notice," *BioScience*, Volume 67, Issue 12, December 2017, Pages 1026–1028, (https://doi.org/10.1093/biosci/bix125).

Ritchie, Hannah and Roser, Max. "Energy Production & Changing Energy Sources." *Published online at OurWorldInData.org*. Retrieved from: https://ourworldindata.org/energy-production-and-changing-energy-sources, 2019.

Robbins, Jim. "Building an Ark for the Anthropocene." *The New York Times*, September 27, 2015.

Romm, Joe. "AGU Scientist Asks, 'Is Earth F**ked'? Surprising Answer: Resistance is Not Futile!" *Thinkprogress.org*, December 9, 2012.

Shabecoff, Philip. "Global Warming Has Begun, Expert Tells Senate." *The New York Times*, June 24, 1988.

Sachs, Jeffrey D. *The Age of Sustainable Development*. New York: Columbia University Press, 2015.

Sack, Kevin and Schwartz, Jonathan. "The Drowning Coast: Left to the Tides and Fighting for Time." *The New York Times* in partnership with *NOLA.Com/The Times-Picayune*, February 25, 2018.

Samenow, Jason. "Two Middle East Locations Hit 129 Degrees, Hottest Ever in Eastern Hemisphere, Maybe the World." *The Washington Post*, July 22, 2016.

Sandalow, David. *Is the Paris Climate Conference Already a Success?* Center on Global Energy Policy, Columbia University, July 14, 2014.

Schiffman, Richard. "Pandemic? Lab Says Main Crisis Is Still Climate." *The New York Times*, April 26, 2020.

Schlossberg, Tatiana. "Rising Sea Levels May Disrupt Lives of Millions, Study Says." *The New York Times*, March 14, 2016.

Schwartz, John. "Energy Options Ebb and Grow: Natural Gas Abundance of Supply and Debate." *The New York Times*, December 23, 2014.

Schwartz, John. "Intolerable Heat May Hit the Middle East by the End of the Century." *The New York Times*, October 26, 2015.

Schwartz, John. "A Milestone for Carbon Dioxide in the Atmosphere." *The New York Times*, October 3, 2016.

Scott, Mark. "Europe Looks Offshore for Power." *The New York Times*, April 23, 2015.

Scripps CO2 Program. *Lessons for Long-Term Earth Observations*. Scrippsco2.ucsd.edu/history, April 15, 2017.

Scripps CO2 Program. *Mauna Loa Observatory, Hawaii: Monthly Average Carbon Dioxide Concentration*. http://scrippsco2.ucsd.edu/data/atmospheric_co2/primary_mlo_co2_record, November 25, 2018.

Sengupta, Somini. "In India, Summer Heat May Soon Be Literally Unbearable." *The New York Times*, July 18, 2018.

Sengupta, Somini. "The Year Global Warming Made Its Menace a Reality." *The New York Times*, August 10, 2018.

Sengupta, Somini. "U.N. Report Says Rise In Emissions Is Still Alarming." *The New York Times*, November 27, 2019.

Sengupta, Somini. "As Earth Heats Up, Inequity Boils Over." *The New York Times*, August 8, 2020.

Schwartz, Mark. "Study: Wind Farms Can Store and Deliver Surplus Energy." *NASA.gov*, March 24, 2014.

Silberg, Bob. "NASA Helps Harness and Ocean of Energy." *NASA.gov*, August 28, 2014.

Slowmoney.org. Various articles, 2015.

The Smithsonian Institution's Human Origins Program (humanorigins.si.edu). *Home sapiens*, August 24, 2018.

Stager, Curt. *Deep Future: The Next 100,000 Years of Life on Earth*. New York: Thomas Dunne Books (St. Martin's Press), 2012.

Strayed, Cheryl. *Wild*. New York: Knopf, 2012.

Stephenson, Wen. "Walking Home From Walden." *Slate.com*, June 21, 2011.

Stern, Nicholas. "The US and China Must Show Leadership on Climate Change." *The Guardian*, December 11, 2013.

Stern, Nicholas. "Climate Change is Here Now and it Could Lead to Global Conflict." *The Guardian*, February 13, 2014.

Stevens, William K. "Yes, You can do something about the Weather." *The New York Times*, December 31, 1996.

Stewart, Heather and Elliot, Larry. "Nicholas Stern: 'I Got it Wrong on Climate Change - it's Far, Far Worse." *The Guardian*, January, 26, 2013.

Stockholm Environmental Institute, A Climate Equity Reference Project Report. *National Fair Shares: The Mitigation Gap - Domestic Action and International Support*, November 12, 2014.

Stromberg, Joseph. "What is the Anthropocene and Are We in It?" *Smithsonian Magazine*, January 2013.

Sullivan, Colin and ClimateWire. "New York City Could See 6-Foot Sea Rise, Tripling of Heat Waves by 2100." *ScientificAmerican.com*, February 19, 2015.

Taylor, Lin. "Food Shortages Due to Climate Change Could Fuel Violence, Unrest: Research." *Reuters.com*, June 9, 2017.

Thompson, Andrea. "Global Warming Key Driver of 2015's Record Heat." *Climatecentral.org*, November 24, 2015.

Thoreau, Henry David. *Walden and On the Duty of Civil Disobedience*.

U.N. Intergovernmental Panel on Climate Change. 2014 report.

U.N. Intergovernmental Panel on Climate Change. *Global Warming of 1.5 degree Celsius: An IPCC Special Report*, October 8, 2018.

United Nations (https://unfcc.int). *UN Warns Climate Change is Driving Global Hunger*, September 12, 2018.

University Corporation for Atmospheric Research. *Global Warming and Climate Change - Frequently Asked Questions*." September 24, 2015.

Urbina, Ian. "A Model for 'Clean Coal' Goes Awry." *The New York Times*, July 5, 2016.

U.S. Department of Defense. "2014 Climate Change Adaptation Roadmap." 2014.

U.S. Energy Information Administration. *eia.gov*, various articles.

U.S. House of Representatives Resolution 109, *Green New Deal*, 116th Congress, 1st Session, February 7, 2019.

U.S. National Park Service (nps.gov). Lincoln Memorial, 2016.

Viacampesina.org. *The International Peasant's Voice*, February 8, 2011.

Viacampesina.org, *Elizabeth Mpofu Speaks Before 50,000 people at the 'We Are Fed Up' Demonstration,* January 21, 2015.

Victor, David D. and Kennel, Charles F. "Climate Policy: Ditch the 2 Degrees Celsius Warming Goal." *Nature.com,* October 1, 2014.

Victor, David. "Climate Change: Embed the Social Sciences in Climate Policy." *Nature.com,* April 1, 2015.

Wallace-Wells, David. *The Uninhabitable Earth: Life After Warming.* New York: Tim Duggan Books (Crown Publishing Group), 2019.

Watts, Geoff. "The cows that could help fight climate change."

(www.bbc.com), August 6, 2019.

Weisman, Alan. "Burning Down the House." *The New York Review of Books,* August 15, 219.

Wiig, O.; Amstrup, S.; Atwood, T.; Laidre, K.; Lunn, N.; Obbard, M.; Regehr, E.; and Thiemann, G. *Ursus Maritimus, The IUCN Red List of Threatened Species 2015.* The International Union for Conservation of Nature and Natural Resources, August 2015.

Willer, Robb. "Is the Environment a Moral Cause?" *The New York Times,* February 27, 2015.

Wilson, Edward O. *A Window on Eternity.* New York: Simon and Schuster, 2014.

Wines, Michael. "Climate Change Threatens to Strip the Identity of Glacier National Park." *The New York Times,* November 22, 2014.

Wiwa, et al v. Royal Dutch Petroleum Company, et al, United States District Court for the Southern District of New York, November 8, 1996, various court documents.

Worldbank.org. *World is Locked into 1.5 degree Celsius Warming & Risks are Rising, New Climate Report Finds.* November 23, 2014.

The World Bank (www.worldbank.org). *4 degrees, Turn Down the Heat: Confronting the New Climate Normal.* 2014

The World Bank (www,worldbank.org). *New Report says Climate Change Could Force Millions to Move Within Their Countries.* March 19, 2018.

The World Health Organization (www.who.int). *Climate Change and Health: Fact Sheet,* updated July 2017.

The World Health Organization (www.who.int). Climate Change and Health, February 1, 2018.

Yee, Amy. "From Ocean Waves, Power and Potable Water." *The New York Times*, April 23, 2015.

Yousafzai, Malala. *I am Malala: The Girl Who Stood up for Education and was Shot by the Taliban.* New York: Little, Brown and Company, 2013.

Zimmer, Carl. "Study Finds Climate Change as Threat to 1 in 6 Species." *The New York Times*, April 30, 2015.

350.org, various articles on its website, 2015-2017.

Additional sources not listed in the bibliography were consulted in 2021 as the book was prepared for publication.

About Author Peter Aronson and his books

Peter is a former lawyer, a former legal-affairs journalist and now a full-time author living in New York City. Peter's major focus so far has been on children's books for middle-grade readers. Peter has written and had published two middle-grade biographies in his Groundbreaker Series, books about extraordinary individuals doing extraordinary things. Both books contain dozens of historic photos.

The first book in the series, published in 2018, was *Bronislaw Huberman: From Child Prodigy to Hero, the Violinist who saved Jewish Musicians from the Holocaust*. Huberman, one of the greatest violinists in the world, used his talents and influence to save Jewish musicians from the Holocaust by starting an orchestra in Palestine in 1936. Saving lives for him became more important than his beloved music. The orchestra he started became the Israel Philharmonic Orchestra, one of the world's great orchestras.

The second book in the series, published in 2019, was *Jeannette Rankin, America's First Congresswoman*. Rankin, who was elected to office in 1916, a full century before Hillary Clinton ran for president, was much more than just a groundbreaking politician. She was a pioneering feminist, suffragette and anti-war activist for decades, outspoken almost until the day she died. She was a true groundbreaker, in every sense of the word.

Both the Huberman and Rankin books are available through Amazon or through Peter's website, www.peteraronsonbooks.com.

In addition, Peter is co-writing a series of soccer novels for middle-grade readers with soccer legend Shep Messing, a member of the 1972 U.S. Olympic soccer team and current broadcaster for the New York Red Bulls. These books will be published in 2022.

Mandalay Hawk's Dilemma: The United States of Anthropocene is Peter's first novel. He wrote it because he believes global warming is the greatest problem humans have ever faced and he truly believes the best way to stop it is for youths to lead the way.

In addition, Peter writes essays, short stories and articles.

For more information, please visit:
www.peteraronsonbooks.com

To communicate with the author:
peteraronsonbooks@gmail.com

Made in United States
North Haven, CT
04 January 2022

14202761R00136